Short Stories (to die for)

J S Langley

First Published in 2019 by

Print ISBN 978-1-9996676-7-2

For Janet, Robert, Iain, Michael

Contents

		Page
1.	The conscientious gardener	7
2.	Affinity for dogs	27
3.	A welcome distraction	45
4.	Remembrance	51
5.	All in the Jeans	55
6.	The saving of Daniel Gray	65
7.	How to make Spaghetti Bolognese	77
8.	Two rooms	93
9.	Surprise, Surprise!	111
10.	The trouble with Catfish	113
11.	Starting out	127
12.	Life and Death	143
13.	Dealing with things	165
14.	Only a game	183
15.	Skin deep	201
16.	Keep on keeping on	205

The conscientious gardener

I like my garden to be orderly, everything in its place, soil analysed, treated and tended. That's the way to get the best produce.

And here I was where I liked to be, in the garden, down on my knees doing some essential weeding. Surrounded by demarcated plots, tailored borders, and burgeoning growth I was in my element. The mange tout were doing well and I was picking the traitorous weeds out of the loose soil very easily. That's the secret you know, the soil, it's quality, texture, alkalinity, fertility. It all needs thinking about.

I know the names of everything in my garden even the weeds, their uses and abuses, their Latin names; *taraxacum officinale,* the humble dandelion for example or *ranunculus acris*, the yellow buttercup.

Each of my plots is managed to suit the crop, rotated to maintain productivity. My next job was to fill the newly dug potato trench with farm manure, delivered earlier in the day in 25kg bags, smelling sweetly. I knew I needed to get it in quickly, to prevent it burning the grass where they sat, piled and steaming, waiting for my attention.

It was at this point that my thoughts were interrupted by a rustling noise.

My garden is surrounded by high, thick hedging, I don't like being overlooked, I don't like to be disturbed. The noise was too loud to be a bird, too clumsy to be one of the local squirrels I was perpetually trapping and disposing of. I ignored it, finished my weeding and made my way to the compost area, an essential part of a successful garden. The sound of a police helicopter caught my attention as it passed slowly overhead, causing me to look up. I shaded my eyes, my fingers coated in good earth. It seemed to be searching for something, completing circles, moving back and forth. I decided to move inside and wait until it went away. I'm not fond of the police and was not seeking to have any interaction with them if I could possibly avoid it.

Not long after I was sitting at my kitchen table, a bowl of the usual cereal swimming in ice cold milk in front of me, a mug of steaming black coffee at my left elbow; two level teaspoonfuls, stirred for 33 seconds counterclockwise.

I was thinking about what I was going to do in the garden later that day, looking forward to it. In my mind's eye I could picture the edges that needed squaring off, the neat rows of seedlings that needed thinning.

These pleasant thoughts were interrupted by an insistent ringing of the front doorbell. Someone was keen to come in. This was annoying particularly as it was very unusual. Nobody rang my doorbell on a Tuesday, urgently or not. I went back to my breakfast, the coffee was now at the perfect temperature for drinking; the buggers could wait, I thought.

I got to the front door just before they started to break it down. I could see them pause as they saw my outline through the frosted glass.

'Police!' shouted an officious voice, 'open the door!'

It was a male voice, full of testosterone, he'd obviously run out of patience.

I unlocked the door.

'We need to search your property, sir, I'm sure you won't mind, it's for your own safety.'

Before I could say that I did mind he'd pushed past me, a second officer following on his bootlaces. Both of them were festooned with bulletproof vests, tasers, real guns and riot helmets, visors up. The second officer immediately ran upstairs. Neither of them took off their dirty boots. I would have to do a deep clean after they'd left.

The first officer took a quick look around the downstairs rooms. As I was being ignored in my own house I went back into the kitchen, sat down at the table and waited. It wasn't long before the first officer reappeared.

'Excuse me sir, but I'll need to look outside in the garden.'

I began to protest but he wasn't listening. The second officer entered and shook his head.

'Upstairs clear,' he said. He seemed disappointed.

The two of them went outside. More mess I thought. I had more than enough work to do harnessing nature's vagaries without tidying up after clumsy policemen. But never mind, it wasn't worth making a fuss about.

After 37 minutes or so the two of them re-entered via the back door. I watched as they paused to wipe their feet on the coconut mat. A bit late for that, I thought.

'May we talk to you, sir,' said the only one of the two who had been granted a voice. It didn't sound like a question.

'Where can we sit?' he asked.

I lead them into the lounge and sat in one of my green leather armchairs. He sat in the other, his dumb colleague stood by the door. A low glass and steel coffee table stood between us like a garden wall, even so I could see that his boots were not perfectly clean.

'I hope you don't mind,' he said, 'I just have one or two questions.'

It was just like the old days, this kind of treatment was bringing back painful memories. He took off his helmet and made himself comfortable. I offered him a cup of tea or something a little stronger. He refused. I saw him glance at my ankle bracelet. The light flashed back a reassuring blue.

They shouldn't have caught me really. One little mistake, or more correctly one unforeseen deluge that flooded a low lying area of wasteland and unearthed a body with traces of my DNA on parts of it. A once in a hundred years event. Most unfortunate. At least they didn't find the others.

I didn't mind prison. Kept myself to myself and, after one of the other inmates was found with a pencil sticking out of his ear, I wasn't troubled by bullying.

I spent my time in the library as much as I could, avoiding the kitchen duties that may have presented me with too many temptations.

Apparently my conduct was increasingly judged as compliant verging on exemplary and I was moved to a more open prison after 4 years 3 months and 6 days and allowed access to outside garden areas.

I was in my element and was slightly peeved when they told me that I'd been assessed as ready for limited release under license back into the community, which amounted to being tagged and put under house arrest.

My Probation Officer, a female PO who put on a show of being friendly, visited me once a week or whenever my tag gave cause for concern, which was hardly ever. If my conduct remained good I was promised increasing levels of freedom, possibly leading eventually to a full release. I didn't really care as long as I had my garden.

Back in the lounge I beat the police officer to his question by answering it.

'House arrest,' I said, knowing that he would know this already, 'I've been released on license.'

'I see,' he said, I wasn't sure that he did, 'but it's not you that brings us here.'

I felt a pang of disappointment, nobody likes to be made to feel unimportant.

'We're looking for someone.'

I'd pretty much guessed that.

'Must be important,' I said, above us I could still hear the sound of the helicopter rotor blades.

The policeman shuffled uncomfortably in his seat.

'Have you seen anybody about?'

I thought about the rustling I'd heard in the thick green leylandii perimeter hedge.

'No,' I said, 'I haven't seen anything, nobody but me and my garden.'

'Are you sure?'

As I've said, I don't like the police and I didn't like the fact that he didn't seem to believe me. Even if I was lying he was still sounding impolite.

'I am,' I said, bristling.

'I'll tell your PO about our visit,' he said.

'Please do,' I said, 'it will save me the job.'

They didn't stay long after that and instead of working in the garden I spent the whole afternoon cleaning up the mess they'd made as they'd clumped around the house.

When it started to get dark I left the French windows and back door to the kitchen unlocked, didn't switch on any lights, and sat in the increasing gloom and waited.

It was gone midnight when I heard a hand at the kitchen door, turning the handle, trying the lock. I could hear the door being pushed slowly open and the careful footfall that followed, though there was no sound of feet being wiped.

'Take off your shoes!' I shouted. I'd done quite enough cleaning for one day.

I thought the surprise might prompt my visitor to bolt, but it didn't.

I went through to the kitchen and turned on the light.

I would guess that the young woman was about 30. Dressed in camouflage gear it was difficult to make out her figure but she seemed to be what you could call “petite”; a little over 5 feet tall, slim, medium looks, probably weighing no more than two sacks of potatoes. Her hair, which appeared to be a natural brunette, was tied back. She was taking off her trainers.

'Take a glass of water,' I said, 'there's food in the fridge, I'll make you a sandwich.'

She laid a sharp looking knife on one of the granite work surfaces and moved to the sink.

'The glasses are in the cupboard, above and to the right,' I said as I proceeded to the fridge and started to prepare the sandwich.

'Is ham, cheese and chutney alright? I wasn't expecting guests so I don't have a lot in.'

'That fine,' she said, her accent thick.

'And I only have white bread.'

'That fine too.'

6 and a half minutes later we sat in the lounge. She was in the same place as the

police officer had occupied earlier. The armchair looked bigger and seemed to almost engulf her in the green of its leather upholstery. The coffee table looked softer, less like a barrier between us.

'So,' I said, 'my name's Brian.' It isn't.

'Mine Lizli,' she said, equally unconvincingly, and proceeded to finish the last of her sandwich, leaving crumbs, and gulped down her third glass of water.

'Dry mouth,' she said.

I let her settle.

'So what do we do now?' I asked.

'We sit a little bit. I tell you a story.'

She laid the knife, sharp steel blade, on the coffee table. There was no doubt who was in charge of this situation.

'I do drugs,' she said.

I was puzzled, she didn't look like an addict, her complexion was far too healthy a colour for that. She noted my reaction.

'Not addict,' she said, 'supplier, one stop shop, tabs, MD, Ket, e, pinger, sniff, heroine, crack, whatever you want, whatever you need, we got it.' She sounded like she was selling fruit and veg from a market stall.

She picked up the knife and waved it threateningly but expertly in the air before replacing it on the toughened glass top of the coffee table.

'I don't mind telling I'm important,' she continued. She may be small in stature, I thought, but not in self confidence or ego, 'spider in centre of web, drug supply, deal, sell, county lines, cuckoo houses.'

It was all probably true, she was clearly someone who warranted an armed police hunt, and helicopters seeking infrared signatures.

She stretched her neck muscles, moving her head from side to side, 'I feel little strange,' she said, 'I not have so much sleep, my business dangerous business.'

She paused and looked around the room.

'Why I tell you this?' she said, it was a question that didn't seem to need an answer.

'Did you enjoy the sandwich?' I asked.

She glanced at the few remaining crumbs that had fallen into her lap.

'The sandwich?' she laughed, 'yes it very nice.'

Then she stopped laughing and looked me straight in the face, I could feel the ice in her eyes.

'I must cover tracks, you understand?'

I looked from her face to the knife, it didn't seem like she was offering to stay the night. No, the threat, or was it a promise, felt very present and very real.

'Sorry,' she said.

'I'm sorry too,' I said.

She tried to move but she couldn't. She looked small, curled and cocooned in the soft leather armchair.

'Feeling strange,' she said.

'It's the chutney,' I said.

'Chutney?'

'Yes, my own special recipe, a mixture of fungi, herbs and flora from my garden, with a strong dash of Belladona, Deadly Nightshade to you and me, those little black berries, so tempting, so dangerous. I'm an expert on these things, I've spent years experimenting, perfecting. You'd be amazed at what you can grow in a suburban garden if you really try. The power of plants is quite extraordinary.'

I could see her straining to move, for the first time there was a glimmer of fear.

'Cramps,' I said, 'creeping paralysis, constricting your muscles, preventing movement. Apparently it's quite painful.'

Her face contorted. Her eyes darted towards the knife, sharp edged and shining, and now out of reach.

'I'm afraid you're not going to be able to kill me. On the contrary,' I said.

I was fairly confident of my chutney's properties so I just left her, with the knife tantalisingly close, and went into the kitchen for a minute or two to get one of the bags I use for the kitchen rubbish bin. There was a possibility she would vomit and I wanted to avoid a mess.

When I returned to the lounge she was lying collapsed on the floor. The knife lay close by, the coffee table overturned. She was obviously a lady of great strength and personal will. I was impressed although I didn't admit it out loud.

Her eyes were fixed and immovable now and stared, wide open, into the middle distance. It was disconcerting.

I placed the bag over her head, the plastic it was made from was biodegradable and it had a tie at the open end that helped with the sealing and lifting process. Designed with the intention of preventing mess during disposal. This was a very useful facet I thought, as I tightened it around the young woman's neck and I filed away this useful fact in my mind for future reference.

She took a further 7 minutes and 49 seconds to die, sucking the bag deeper into her windpipe in her desperation to breathe. She did not vomit though, a sign of her presence of mind to the last. I was proud of her.

Without switching on any of the outside lights I brought the wheelbarrow up to the French windows, no point overstraining myself. Executing a near perfect fireman's lift I carried her from the lounge, through the French windows and into the wheelbarrow.

The rest was easy.

I'd already dug my potato trench. I already had my pile of manure.

Before burying her completely I used the garden fork to ensure she was dead. I'm not a monster. I have my standards. Burying someone alive was an abhorrent idea to me.

The blood oozed black in the night as it poured out and into the soil. I poked a few more times just to make sure, the iron would be good for the soil, the calcium from the bones would be good as well but would be more of a slow release.

I piled more manure, garden compost and soil on top. With this combination I was hopeful of growing prize potatoes and hoped by the time they were ready I may have earned enough privileges to enter them in a local produce show. I wasn't too bothered about DNA contamination this time. This garden wasn't on a flood plain and good luck to anybody who tried untangling any part of this body from all the faeces and other organic matter and extracting a DNA sample that would be suitable to put before a jury.

When I'd finished the heavy stuff it was after 2 in the morning. I decided to leave it there and get some sleep. I knew that between the coming sunrise and sunset I had the time to tidy up both inside and out, removing any stray hairs from the armchair and floor, obscuring wheelbarrow tracks, clearing stray soil, compost and manure from the lawn. I would enjoy that, I like tidying.

The next time my PO came round I found myself sitting opposite her in the same lounge, the same armchairs, the same coffee table. It was a strange sensation. Policeman, drug dealer, PO; same place, same chairs, different purposes, different outcomes.

She noticed me smiling.

'How are things going?' she asked.

I thanked her for the shopping she'd brought round; the fresh bread, the breakfast cereal, the vinegar for making some more chutney... and then I told her about the police but not about my other visitor.

'I know,' she said, I figured she would, 'pretty much a waste of time and tax payer's money as far I understand it.'

I wasn't so sure. We talked about my gardening. A subject of endless interest and fascination to me.

'Did the manure arrive OK?' she asked eventually.

'Yes thanks. Arrived, mixed with lawn clippings and dead leaves, applied, and dug in. Now I'm looking forward to the results. Good compost is the lifeblood of a garden you know, and I pride myself on its preparation.'

'I see,' she said, giving the appearance of starting to lose interest. She would probably have paid more attention if she'd known more about some of the ingredients, the more biological components, rich in iron and calcium.

She looked at my ankle brace.

'At our next review I'm going to recommend you for the next stage of release into the community. Because of your previous psychopathic tendencies we'll have to keep monitoring you I'm afraid but I think we should give you more freedom to move about independently, do your own shopping, observe a curfew, that kind of thing. How does that sound?'

By 'previous psychopathic tendencies' she meant the suspicion I was still under of being a serial killer. They'd only found one body and that was only by a fluke of nature. The others were buried more securely and unlikely to come to light, most of the produce they'd fertilised would have been well consumed by now. Anyway I'd probably done society a favour with this last one.

'That sounds good,' I said noncommittally.

She seemed surprised at my lack of enthusiasm. But what use were further privileges if everything I needed just kept coming to me?

Affinity for dogs

Tuesdays are the worst for me.

Whatever pleasure there may have been in the previous weekend has long since shrivelled, dried brown and blown away in the breeze. The prospect of the next weekend seems so far away that no matter how far I stretch out my arms I can't touch it; not even with the tips of my fingers. And anyway it's difficult to be 'creative on demand' on any day of the week; never mind a Tuesday.

I sat at my electronic drawing board doodling.

'We don't care how you do it but come up with something,' they'd said, 'something fabulous,' and then, as if as an afterthought, 'Oh yes, and by Friday,' pause, 'earlier if you'd like!'

Advertising; it's a pain in the ass. Well I ask you, what 'fabulous' thing was I going to be able to conjure up about a dog food that hadn't been conjured up, dissected, repackaged and regurgitated several hundred times already? OK, I do spend some volunteer time at a dog's home so there was some sense, some, in giving this assignment to me. In fact, no matter whether they're big, small, hairy, fat or thin, dogs do seem to take to me. I think I have what you would call a mutual affinity with dogs. On the other hand this doesn't give me any special access into a dog's sensory preferences and besides, as far as I know, dogs don't read advertising literature, are not swayed by slick ads and don't drool over snappy slogans. In my experience most dogs just wolf down whatever you put in front of them.

What I was in need of was some form of inspiration and I knew from past experience that there was one approach that seemed to work for me. I had to get up and out of the overpowering, magnetically attractive seat that I occupied routinely for 6-8 hours Monday to Friday and had managed to mould to the individual undulations of my increasingly wayward posterior, and hit the road Jack; get out there into the real world. Fresh air, green trees; smooch about, soak in the minutiae of other people's everyday lives, let it swirl and cogitate and hope that something would trigger an alchemic spark and another prize winning campaign would emerge; as if by magic. Not that I'd had any previous prize winning campaigns mind you but that's only because of the short-sighted arrogance of the over-rated pretentious morons that they call judges - I'm not bitter.

I'm not old either, but I would admit to no longer being frivolously adolescent; and I'm definitely not bordering on desperate like some of my so-called 'friends' say, mainly behind my back I'm pleased to say. I don't think I'm obese (what a horrible word) though I do have a healthy covering - nothing that a couple of days in the gym couldn't sort out - if only I could find the time. I have honed my dress sense to an individual form of idiosyncratic and get a lot of comments about that - some of which I don't know how to take.

From a personality perspective, which is much more important than the superficial veneer of temporal looks, the label that has most seemed to stick is 'laid back'. My boss once said to me during one of those tiresome annual appraisal interviews 'Debs, if you were any more laid back you'd be horizontal' and then he'd laughed at his own joke. I remember vaguely wondering if I could get him for being sexist but I couldn't be bothered to pursue it.

If I'm honest I don't really think I'm that laid back but I do think I'm not quite normal. Like when my own mother died for instance, a traumatic event in anybody's life, but I just didn't react like I expected myself to. My feelings seemed suppressed, dampened. I just felt kind of disconnected, as if I were watching myself from afar. Like I was me but I was living my own life at a distance somehow and wasn't completely in control of what I was doing, not behaving quite like the real me did, not even shedding a tear. I even went for checks and the best they could come up with was something called Derealisation/Depersonalisation Disorder, shortened to DDPD to make it sound more defined. Didn't make much sense to me, and I decided it was best just to get on with it, so I stopped going. They didn't seem to mind, nobody contacted me when I just failed to show up for appointments.

Anyway, time was a-wasting so I put on my coat, leaving it to hang open, hooked my life-essentials containing bag over my shoulder, waved to my fellow office slaves and headed into the outside.

The first thing I immersed myself in was the life-stream of people that thronged the big city streets. When you need to think it's really good to get distracted; let your conscious mind cope with a deluge of images and colours flashing past, in and out of view, your body physically dodging around fellow jaywalkers who are jostling their own way to god knows where, for god knows what, whilst the unconscious mind whirs silently away in the background, uncoupled and unfettered by it's annoying neighbour. Well that's my theory anyway. I'm also fond of an amount of shopping therapy and quickly dodged in and out of a few of my favourite stores, trying things on I didn't need and couldn't afford before buying some extra knickers and tights (you can never have too many of them) and studiously avoiding the glorious display of boots and shoes that were on a special - who said I had no willpower.

Re-emerging temporarily consumer satiated, but without the inspiration I was seeking, I cursed my inner self's inability to function to order and decided that it was the peace of more open spaces that I needed: the green of the countryside, the blue of wide horizons.

I didn't have the time or energy to go too far so a walk around the local park would have to do. The exercise, in any case, would do me good.

The black painted cast iron gate was pitted with the years and ground on its un-oiled hinges as I pushed through the dividing line between urban and rural. Once released it sprung back into its allotted place, alive on coiled springs that were taut to their task and nearly trapped my unsuspecting fingers. As I started to walk down one of the winding paths, feeling the gritted surface scrunch beneath my feet, I had an uneasy feeling that all was not well. I don't know what it was but I felt like I was being watched, the subject of unfriendly scrutiny. Looking around however I could see that therc were only one or two other people about ; a couple sitting on the grass entwined, a jogger in over-tight Lycra of bright yellow and blue that didn't suit, and a guy walking his two dogs, pulling on their leads. I shrugged off the feeling as an expression of a normal and healthy level of paranoia and continued my wander, inspiration having not yet descended upon me.

It was not an unpleasant day, there was some blue showing between the clouds and the clouds themselves were whiter than the heavy grey that is the harbinger of heavy rain. Being a Tuesday nothing much was happening; kids were at school, parents at work, and it was the mid-afternoon lull. This lack of unnecessary distraction was just what I needed to slip into a meditative daydreaming state although my calm was spoilt by the nagging question of whether I'd closed the kitchen window before leaving my apartment for work. Nevertheless I wandered aimlessly but contentedly around and across the green spaces, along the side of the lake, even investing in a small cone of ice cream, with raspberry sauce. If this didn't bring me a breakthrough nothing would, I thought, as I meandered away from the lake and towards the more wooded areas.

The majesty of ancient oak climbed high above an under canopy of coppiced hazel a woodland reminder of a time when we used to grow our building materials, farm our forests.

It was as I was walking along the edge of this woodland, lost in my own thoughts, that the dog walker caught up with me; big guy, muscular, long hair, t-shirt, slacks and trainers, he was holding the dogs' leads tightly in one gigantic hand.

'You like me dogs,' he said, out of the blue.

I hadn't looked at his dogs. I did now. I know my dogs and these were clearly a cross between rottweiler and pit bull, all muscle and teeth.

'Very nice,' I said.

He looked down at them adoringly. 'I love me dogs,' he said, 'and they love me.' He pointed to each in turn 'This is Nero, and this little beauty is Sabina, the love of his life. There's plenty waiting for pups from these two I can tell you.'

An acquired taste, I thought, looking into their slobbering, drooling, dribbling jaws.

'I keep ‘em underfed,' he continued proudly, ' "Treat 'em mean and keep 'em keen" that's what I always says.'

He paused to look around and then turned back.

'Just like me women,’ he said and grabbed at me with his free hand.

This sudden change from the every-day mundane to the frighteningly physical took me completely by surprise and off balance. He dropped the dog's leads and manhandled me into the wood, the dogs following obediently at his heels. I should have screamed, 1 know I should have screamed, but something in me just froze. I'd somehow, in an instant, stopped being a sentient human being and had become just meat, prey. He turned me backwards, put his big coarse hand over my useless mouth and dragged me into the cover of the trees, my heels bouncing over uneven, broken, boulder strewn ground.

'Oh, you're a good one,' he said, 'this is going to be good.'

My popping eyes stared down at the two under-nourished dogs obediently following their master, tongues out, panting.

It all went so fast from there. At some point he must have thought we were sufficiently off the beaten track because he stopped dragging me and threw me to the ground under a hazel, my bag flying off my shoulder, and shifted position so that he was on top of me.

I didn't react like I expected. I didn't defend myself in the way that I should have done. It was almost like I was looking at myself, shouting in my own ear to struggle, scratch, not just lay back as my legs were forced open. What was it that he was saying? I just saw his lips move, couldn't hear the words, saw the crooked leer on his face, the cracked teeth. It was like I was looking down on me, me lying there, me with my legs open. I had my legs open. Did I have my legs open? I can't remember clearly, but it was me I was looking at. I was sure of that. Move you idiot! Put up a fight!

It must have been only seconds, though it felt a lot longer, when at last some of my senses returned and as he reached down to loosen his belt and pull down his trousers I pushed myself upwards and backwards on my elbows and then onto my knees, onto my feet, into low branches, my weight and fear-fuelled strength pushing into them, hard. Large branches, I don't know how large, coiled with my stored energy.

He laughed and pulling up his pants crouched and came at me.

I didn't mean to do it, it wasn't on purpose, but as I went down for the second time a branch I'd leant on sprung back over my head like a whip, catching him on the side of the head, smashing into his right temple. On its own it wouldn't have been that effective but he was off balance and as he fell he twisted and smashed the back of his head, the soft part at the base, on one of the boulders that protruded sporadically through the detritus of the forest floor.

He gave out a kind of gurgled groan and a dark liquid started to spread from beneath his hair. The dogs growled and came toward me. I kept very still so as not to appear a threat and tried to control the shaking in my head, my arms, hands, legs.

The dogs sniffed and snuffled in my face, dropping slaver. Nero barked. I held my nerve. Sabina growled. Steady, steady I repeated in my head, steady. Nero opened his jaws, wide. I smelt his acid breath. His eyes dropped to mine.

It seemed like an age.

He looked away, shook his head, yawned, and turned, and trotted to where his owner lay.

Sabina followed him and I watched their muscled hind quarters, their discarded dog leads trailing along behind them, as they bent to the ground.

It was all like a dream, a bad dream.

The dogs started licking.

'I love 'em and they love me.' A confused version of his words was rattling around in my head.

The taste of blood did something to them. Their bodies tensed.

'I keep 'em underfed. Treat 'em mean to keep 'em keen.'

Nero started to chew. Sabina growled and pushed for her own place. Crunching sounds brought me back to life. The two dogs were tearing, pulling and gnawing now.

I got onto my hands and knees and started to crawl away. Finding the strap of my bag I pulled it to me, like a lost friend.

Around me the trees were a blur, all I could feel was the moss, the stones, the sticks beneath my hands as I scrabbled forward, sharp edges digging into my knees, the pain giving me a renewed sense of reality. I followed the light, searching for a sky not obscured by the tangled branches of waving trees. I don't know how long it took but I just kept crawling, panting until eventually I felt a wider space and realised I had, thankfully, thank god, reached the edge of the wood and was looking over a redemptive heaven of flat green.

Slowly I pulled myself vertical, ascending, evolving, from ape to human.

I stood and tried to re-ground myself, deliberately brushing away, piece by piece, the debris from hair and fabric, cleansing myself.

I'm not very good at tidying up my own mess never mind anybody else's so I headed off and left it for others to sort out. I was sure that it was only a matter of time before Police, Ambulance, RSPCA would be involved. I was happy to leave it to the professionals. My body was tingling from head to toe, my steps still a little unsteady, my legs shaking.

I headed for a coffee bar and went straight to the toilets. Dipping down into the depths of my bag I found those little bits of essential makeup, half used and out of date, that I always carried and together with soap and warm water I put my face back together and sponged down those areas of clothing that needed it. It didn't take long and when I looked in the mirror I saw what looked like me looking back, worse for wear but recognisable. Only my coat needed more work, the stains on the back were too deep, one of the pockets was torn. But this was OK, I could carry it folded, over my arm, nobody would notice.

Knowing something about the effects of shock I bought myself a sweet tea, sat in the corner and wept. You can do this in a big city without being disturbed, none of the 'are you alright pet?' or even worse 'how can I help?' that you get up North. I'm a strong woman, I can handle my own problems thank you very much. I hoped the dogs would not be destroyed.

I took my time. My mind was going over the facts, sorting, sifting, deleting -sorting, filing, compartmentalising.

After all it's not every day you see an attempted rapist eaten by his own dogs.

I'd watch the local News but my guess was that it would all be seen as a tragic accident. A trip, a fall, over-hungry fighting dogs, a shame, what was left of the body would be removed, a report would be written, everything would be tidied up, no nonsense, an open and shut case, tick the boxes, move on. Good job he'd pulled his pants back up, might have begged some extra, unwelcome questions. I'd keep out of it if I could. I'd deal with the flashbacks myself, get help only if I needed it, stay in control of my own destiny.

I wonder who he was.

The whole thing was already feeling unreal. If I did hear it on the news would that cement it into reality or would I fail to recognise I'd been there? Then again there was so much bad news maybe this incident wouldn't even get a by-line. I should be reacting more emotionally, this should be traumatic, but I just wasn't feeling it, I was more concerned about the job in hand.

Back in the office I sat back at my desk, people were already beginning to get restive, it wasn't long before we all 'clocked off'. I'd already decided that the best thing to do was not to tell anybody about what had happened. I would have to discipline myself when I was out with the girls and had perhaps partaken of a smidgen more alcohol than was good for me but I was up for that challenge. Even if I let something slip chances were that they wouldn't believe me, they were used to my exaggerated tales.

Thankfully I had avoided looking at the more grisly sights and it was only the memory of some of the sounds that might be a bit difficult to come to terms with. I could have called for help I suppose, but I don't think it would have made much difference. If he'd wanted that he should have attacked somebody with a bit more 'umph' than me shouldn't he, it was his own fault.

It was while I was watching the clock and mulling things over that an idea popped into my conscious mind. I don't know if you can call it inspired, but it would do, it would take the pressure off the next few days. I tapped at the keys and saw the words appearing on the screen,

'Your best friend need cleaner teeth, fresher breath, stronger jaws?

Try “Affinity” doggy treats – for dogs who love their owners and bought by owners who love their dogs.’

A welcome distraction

Crowded cruise ship embarkation lounges are terrific places for thieves.

They are also cathedrals of boredom and I'd already lost track of the time I'd been sitting waiting there surrounded by my own baggage, minding my own business, a young couple on my right, a more aged one on my left, me on my own in the middle.

Following signs and listening to the odd, barely audible, announcement over the antique PA system had given me some reassurance that I was in the right place and that all was in fact well. As long as I remained patient then further announcements, expected 'soon', would guide me on my way to the next queuing point.

I am not a patient man.

Already the normal pleasantries you exchange with strangers that share your predicament had been exhausted.

The 'Have you travelled far?', 'Wasn't the traffic horrendous ... have you been on a cruise ship before?', 'Oh, really, where to ... who with ... how long?' conversations had run their torturous course and reached the port of 'uncomfortable silence'. My pretence at searching my phone for non-existent urgent texts/emails/messages from 'the Office' or from my nearest and dearest was also wearing thin so it was with some relief that I spotted a young man casually take a handbag whilst its owner was looking the other way, oblivious to the loss.

I turned to my left.

'Could you keep an eye on my bags? I need the men's room.'

'Sure, take your time, seems like we'll be waiting a long while yet.'

'Thanks'

I got up and followed my target. He was a cool customer, making his way slowly towards the exit as if he'd just seen off his granny. I caught up with him and pushed him into a quiet corner between a wall and one of the many food and drinks vending machines.

'What the ...!' he said.

'I don't think that's yours,' I said, nodding to the bulge under his waterproof outer jacket.

'Get off me,' he hissed.

I needed him to take me seriously so I slipped my left hand between his legs and squeezed his testicles in friendly greeting. I've found this to be a much more effective way of galvanizing a young man's attention than shaking hands or saying 'Hi'.

'What the f...' he spat through clenched teeth.

'Do you want to keep these?' I asked, giving them a tweak. He winced, 'Now you listen to me, and listen carefully. Take out that lady's handbag and give it to me. Then you can leave. Understand.'

I squeezed harder. He nodded.

'Slowly,' I said.

I backed slightly away, retaining my grip but giving him a little room. He unzipped the front of his jacket, pulled out the bag.

'Now just drop it on the floor.'

He did so.

'You bastard,' he said, 'I'll rip your

fucking head off for this.'

Maybe it was the pain getting to him but he should have realised that he was not in a position to be issuing threats.

'Back away and leave,' I said, releasing my grip to his evident relief.

His hands went immediately to his pounding parts and then, with a snarl, he tried to head butt me.

Here I was trying to be a gentleman, giving this young man a little lesson in the hopes of nudging him back onto the straight and narrow, helping him to see the error of his ways, and this was the thanks I got. I was a bit peeved.

His lunge put him off balance and the sharp of my knee met the softness of his stomach and winded him. I pushed him backwards banging the back of his head against the wall. He slid slowly down to the floor now pliantly unconscious and I laid his head against the side of the vending machine, he looked as if he was sleeping.

The whole exchange had taken only a minute or two - in a crowded, noisy lounge I hoped that we had not attracted unwelcome attention. As far as I could see we hadn't.

A grey-haired lady approached and started feeding coins into the vending machine. She glanced at the recumbent youth.

'The youngsters of today,' I said, 'they just can't stand the pace.'

She smiled and carried on with the coin feeding, hoping to win a coffee.

I took a circuitous route back and slipped the handbag back into its original place. The victim of the theft was still in deep conversation with her neighbours, completely oblivious of the whole episode.

I regained my seat.

'Thanks' I said.

'No problem. This waiting is so boring isn't it. We could do with something to distract us - make the time go a bit faster.'

I could only agree.

Remembrance

I stand by the white rectangular upright stone. The sky is blue today and I believe I can feel the warmth of the sun on my face.

A middle-aged woman enters the cemetery. Despite the heat she has a coat tight-hugged around her, as if to give comfort. She makes her way along the parallel rows of frozen stone. She carries a piece of white paper in her hand and checks her notes against the number of the row and counts inward. As she passes the graves she takes time to read the rank, name, age and date of death of some of the many who are buried here.

Now she walks slowly towards me. She is in front of me. She stops. I look into her face and believe I recognize something familiar, a likeness to an image in a sepia-faded photograph.

'16993, Private J. H. Higgins, West Yorkshire Regiment, 4th June 1916, 21 years old,' she reads, 'Killed on the Somme, a long way from home.'

The sounds of her spoken words are alive, they reverberate around me and trigger memory.

There is a pain to this memory. I close my eyes and see again the all-clinging brown mud of the trench. I smell the days-old putrefaction that surrounds me. On either side, and more immediate, I see the butchered poppy-red remnants of what were, only seconds ago, fellow human beings. I hear the incessant screaming thunder of the guns and feel the ground shake it's angry reply.

A whistle blows and I see myself scramble untidily over the top of the trench wall, through the barbed wire. I hear the zip, zip of bullets around me and hear the frightened cries of the freshly wounded. Then I am lost in my own pain. I reach out, but my own blackness engulfs me.

A pause, to let the darkness clear, and I am back at my station by the white stone. I re-open my eyes to see that a smart man in a suit is now standing alongside the woman, his arm around her shoulders.

'This is the one,' she says, 'this is my granddad.'

I see a tear form in the corner of her eye. It builds and overflows, rolling silently down her cheek, smudging her make-up. I let go of my rifle, let drop the ammunition pouches and the Mills bombs, the rapier-sharp bayonet and reach forward to wipe away that tear.

I have waited such a long time.

She kneels and is quiet for a moment. Then she leans forward, stretches out a hand and trails her fingers along the cold whiteness, the sharp indentations of the carved lettering on the headstone, strokes them gently across the engraved name.

We touch.

As she gets to her feet our eyes meet unseeingly across the generations and she smiles.

'I'm glad I came,' she says.

All in the Jeans

'So dad,' I said nudging him into wakefulness, 'How's life?'

The sun was already beating down on his bald dome of a cranium determined to turn it a cooked lobster red. It was one of those balmy English summer mornings, so rare and yet so precious.

He was in his garden, a large manicured lawn stretched before us, merging into trees and green and browns and blue. Swallows swooped overhead chirring to one another, catching flies.

My father opened his eyes slowly, turned his head and brought me into focus. I felt like a child again.

'I'm fine,' he said. Nothing more, just 'I'm fine' and then he stopped, silent, waiting. He was an expert at disconcerting me, always had been. It was one of the things I didn't like about him, never had done, for as long as I could remember.

'I was just remembering Marmy,' I said, using the faux American accent that I knew he hated. He stiffened.

'What do you mean?' he said.

'I mean about when and how she died. I keep having dreams, they wake me up at night.'

'What kind of dreams?'

'It's always the same,' I said, 'I see myself in bed. I'm restless, tossing and turning, and then I wake up. I need the toilet. I push back the sheets and get out of bed. I open the bedroom door, turning the cold brass knob, pushing the door open, and then I start to walk down the corridor, on my way to the toilet ...'

My father interrupted me,

'Why now?' he said, 'it's 25 years since your mother, my Jean, died.'

There were tears in his eyes. He never cried. I must have imagined it.

'I was 4 or 5 I think,' I said, ignoring him, 'and in my dream I'm at the top of some stairs and I hear shouting, and I'm scared and the shouting gets louder, and I think it's my mother's voice.'

He stretched out his hand, pointing, 'It's down there,' he said, 'under that old oak tree. That's where we spread her ashes. It's a long time ago, another lifetime.'

'Why did you kill her?' I asked.

He wasn't shocked. He just seemed not to hear.

'After your mother died I tried my best to give you a good home ...'

Oh yes, I remember, I thought, lots of nannies and 'aunties' and boarding schools.

'I gave you a solid foundation. She'd have been proud of you, a son who's now a medical man, respected, professional ... stable.'

'Why did you kill her?'

'A married man. A man with his own Jean,' he smiled, 'a father with his own son.'

'Why?'

'It was just a tragic accident, nobody's fault. That was the legal opinion. She must have slipped, fallen in the kitchen and banged her head.'

'I heard you arguing.'

'I came home later, found her on the floor in a sea of her own blood. Terrible. Tragic.'

'I heard you.'

'I rang the ambulance as soon as I found her. They arrived quickly, did what they could, took her away.'

'I heard.'

'She never regained consciousness, never spoke another word. DoA the hospital said - Dead on Arrival. I stayed in the house because you were there, couldn't leave you on your own. Didn't touch anything because I knew the police were on their way.

'You.'

'The most difficult thing was trying to explain things to you,' he looked at me in sadness, 'it's not easy explaining to an infant that his mother is gone.'

'But the police never talked to me, never asked if I'd seen or heard anything.'

'But you didn't, did you? You're talking about dreams, fantasies, nothing real. The shock must have triggered your imagination, caused some unconscious reaction.'

'I don't believe you.'

'It was 25 years ago, why bring it up now? You've never talked to me like this before.'

'You've never been frail enough and I've never been bold enough to tell you that I know. But I want you to know, before you die I want you to know, and I want you to know that I hate you for it.'

A frail, bald, creased old shell of a man he sat hunched in his wheelchair. The strong man that I had been afraid of, the man who had towered over me, blotting out my sun, was gone. Cancer had got him, eating into his body as he had eaten into my soul. It wouldn't be long now. We both knew it.

He sighed, looked around, looked up imploringly.

'Yes,' he said.

'Yes what?'

'I have my limits, I have my standards. Always have done. Things to live by.'

'And...?'

'Jean was a different person after we got married, after you were born.'

Another, final, dig - I was at fault for being born was I? Born 8 months after the wedding, you tell me who misbehaved. At that time, in that age, I was called 'premature'.

'Go on.'

'She was very possessive, didn't understand a man's needs. I tried to cope.'

You tried to cope!

'But by our 5th wedding anniversary I realised that I had all I needed; a respected position, a nice house, a son. Jean was no longer a necessary component in my life but she had the power to take all these things away from me.'

He'd always been a logical thinker. That's one of the few things I got from him.

'That couldn't be allowed. I tried to explain but she just didn't get it. I suppose being about to die clouded her judgement.'

He didn't need to say anymore. I could fill in the gaps.

'I hope you die soon,' I said, trying to hurt him.

'Me too,' he replied.

I left him sitting in the sun and walked back through the house, past his carer.

'I'm so pleased you could visit. Your father is being so brave but ...'

Hcr pausc driftcd into nothingncss, just like he would, the sooner the better.

'The sun is quite strong,' I said, 'I think his head is beginning to burn.'

'Of course,' she said, and stepped on towards the garden, 'I'll find him some shade.'

Murder after 5 years married. I drove home. As I turned into our lane I saw another car pulling out of the drive of my house. Passing the bespoke wrought iron gates my Merc made a reassuring crunching sound on the gravel surface. I parked up, got out and walked to my front door. I was a little earlier than expected. I opened the front door and went inside.

'Hi Jean,' I shouted as I entered the spacious hall. It was a nice house.

She came to the top of the stairs and looked down at me, dressed in a red silk kimono embroidered in yellow, black and green. She'd bought that for herself. I would never buy her anything like that. She looked dishevelled.

'Oh hello dear,' she said, 'I haven't been feeling too well this morning. Lawrence is at my parents for the day, they came and picked him up. You know how they love to spoil him.'

Who wouldn't want to spoil our boisterous 3 year old boy?, I thought. But then again this seemed like too much information too quickly.

'Who was it I saw pulling out of the drive?' I asked as calmly as I could.

There was only a flicker of hesitation. You had to know her to see it at all.

'That was just a man from the kitchen suppliers. He came to measure up so they can give us a quote. I just let him in and left him to it.'

Ah yes, of course, another new kitchen refit. An annual event.

'I think I'll go for a shower,' she continued, 'maybe it'll make me feel better, brighten me up a bit.'

I watched as she turned her back on me and disappeared into the upper recesses of the house. Our nice house, nice just as it was.

We'd been married about 3½ years now, Lawrence was a 'honeymoon baby'. I could manage another 2 years, get thc boy off to school. And then when it was necessary, and it would be necessary, I wouldn't make such a drama out of it. No shouting. Lawrence safely out of the house. I wouldn't want that bit of history to repeat itself. As a medical man I had been trained in ways and means of doing things quietly. I'm not like my father.

'Enjoy your shower,' I shouted up the stairs, 'I'll go and open a bottle of Chardonnay.'

The saving of Daniel Gray

His mouth full of dribbling, white foaming, mint tasting toothpaste the man spluttered, 'The name's Gray, Daniel Gray,' at his own reflection in the mirror. He rinsed and spat.

'Gray by name and grey by nature,' he added, and reached for the dental floss.

Daniel Gray was a middle-aged podgy man who was very particular about his appearance. In fact he was pernickety in every aspect of his life and was proud to have achieved the social status commensurate with his achievement of an ONC in Accountancy.

The alarm had sounded at 7:07 a.m, as it did each weekday morning, and he was dressing, as he dressed every morning, Monday to Friday.

He stooped to pull up the dark grey sharp-creased trousers and fastened them at the waist with a brown crocodile skin effect plastic belt that had a base metal gold-plated lookalike buckle. Over his head he wafted a crisp white shirt. In went the amber cufflinks followed by the careful knotting of a subdued tone mock-silk tie. Polished brown brogues were then shoehorned over Christmas present paisley patterned socks. A grey jacket, colour matching the trousers, was shrugged over his shoulders and all the while Daniel looked admiringly at himself in the full length mirror that was one of his treasures.

'You up yet? Come down and get your breakfast!'

Daniel still lived with his mother. He liked to think that this was his sacrifice although he knew his mother thought that it was hers. She believed she was still looking after him and treated him like the 8 year old boy she wished him still to be.

'Coming mother!'

Daniel completed his dressing artificially slowly in a show of minor every-day rebellion to his mother's urgent summons. He eyed his writing desk that sat by the window on which were a few leaves of his work-in-progress literary masterpiece "Seven ways to murder your Mother and get away with it". He was busy researching No. 2.

Stacked neatly on bookshelves that stood either side of the desk was his library of books. They were all logically ordered and arranged alphabetically by author and category. One shelf held titles such as "Naturally occurring poisons", "Cannibalism in the 21st century" and Robert Graves' "The death of the Gorgon". In his mind's eye he pictured his mother downstairs, small, boney, wrinkled and wizened, arthritically stooped. A great hairy wart on the end of her nose she was leaning over a green-smoking cauldron and cackling as she added eye of newt, bladder of toad, sting of wasp to the evil brew, chanting as she stirred the broth to a bubbling foment.

'Are you coming, it's getting cold!'

'OK Mother, on my way.'

Daniel sighed as he glanced at the rows of James Bond books and beneath them, the carefully compiled volumes of Spiderman, Superman, Batman and Green Lantern comics he'd collected painstakingly over the years. His eyes travelled below these again to the weekly comics he'd collected like "Lion", "Victor", and "Eagle" and he remembered fondly that, as a young boy, it was the Lion that he, Daniel, had habitually taken to his den, under the bed, when he needed to escape.

The breakfast he sat down to at the kitchen table, was not cold. The bacon was crisp, the yoke of the fried egg was runny, the white toast was lightly browned. All was just as he liked it. All was just as it was every morning. He ate in silence as his mother gave him a rundown of the extraordinary happenings in her favourite daytime soaps. She was addicted to daytime TV and loved to recount the deaths and doom-laden events in the TV soap operas she watched.

'Two more goners yesterday,' she said, 'and the cat choked trying to swallow a diamond ring that was a love gift to a Jezebel from Ferdinand, who is a bit of a devil, and is married to Bertha but is unhappy and jealous of just about everyone. Mirabelle fell off a cliff whilst birdwatching. Very unfortunate, can't trust a Puffin, that's what I say.'

Daniel let the words flow over him, nodding occasionally. He never listened to this litany of disaster, instead his mind drifted past the gossip and slander, the yellow yolk and the buttered toast and back upstairs to his bookshelves.

Peter Parker, Clark Kent. These were his heroes and his hope. Proof that you could be two things, not one, even if the superheroes he idolised were not as much in touch with their feminine side as he was. He, Daniel Gray, also had a secret identity. Right now he had to admit that it was all his own secret and that nobody was interested in it. But that, he knew, was only a matter of time.

It was a Monday and Mondays at the Tax office were very predictable, as were most other days. Daniel got to his desk at 8:58 a.m. Gary the office wag asked him if he had had a fun weekend, accompanying the question with various innuendos associated with his latest lascivious exploits and calling him 'Danny-boy' to a background of familiar giggles and sniggers from the open office audience.

Daniel answered, 'Fine, thanks. Very quiet,' as he always did, whilst fantasising on selecting the most painful torture from a shelf of painful tortures that he would like to inflict on Gary's testicles. In reality though, he smiled, fetched himself his first cup of coffee of the day, sat back at his desk, and prepared himself to endure another Monday.

After work Daniel took a detour to the Oxfam shop and got there when there was still 21 minutes to closing. He perused the ranks of second-hand clothes, running the materials between the tips of his fingers, taking garments from their hangers to examine them more closely, occasionally taking sidelong glances into the half length mirror that hung on the shop wall.

'I'll take these,' he said, passing an armful of clothes to a middle-aged lady whose hair was dyed blue.

She looked at him askance.

'For my mother,' he explained.

She smiled, 'We do have smaller sizes,' she said helpfully.

'These are fine. Mother likes to have things loose fitting. Besides, she can take them in if she wants to.'

'Would you like a cup of tea?' his mother asked over her shoulder as he walked in through the front door.

'No thanks,' said Daniel, and she nodded and turned back to the TV, engrossed in an Australian soap.

Up in his room Daniel slipped casually into the purple-velvet slinky number he had picked up at the Oxfam shop. It made him feel more relaxed. He stood in front of the full-length mirror and admired the way the long length dress hugged his still taut buttocks. He put on a pair of high heels that extended and tightened his calf muscles and showed them off at their best. He made a mental note that it was again time to shave his legs. He turned, pirouetted. He liked what he saw. He was no longer Daniel Gray, ONC Accountancy, he was ...

He paused in thought, ruminating, checking the feel of the name, rolling it around in his head, considering the texture, ensuring that it suited his alter ego as well as the clothes suited his figure. Yes he thought, no longer the grey, cowardly, dull, Daniel Gray - now the flamboyant, lively, adrenaline charged ... Glamour-man!

All he needed now, as all superheroes need, was a super villain against which he could match his wits and his powers (although he wasn't quite sure yet what these were). A super villain that had some dastardly plot against humanity that he, at great personal risk, would be the only one capable of countering. To be fair, he'd been waiting some time.

The next day, Tuesday, came and went as did its midweek successor, Wednesday, without the slightest variation, perturbation or fluctuation in the monotony that he felt was his current life. On Thursday, whilst everyone else was out at lunch, he was sitting at his desk enjoying the quiet. He glanced at the clock, it was 12:02hrs and in precisely 5 minutes he knew that he would be relieved and that he would rise from his chair, go to the sandwich shop on the corner of Wise Street and Morecambe Road and order a tuna salad baguette, a packet of organic crisps and a small bottle of mineral water. It would cost him precisely three pounds and twenty-five pence, including VAT, as long as there were no surprise price increases.

It was so unexpected that at first he did not notice the middle-aged woman flounce into the office. Bleach blonde, large bosomed and flowered dress, she looked around, spotted him, and bounded over, teeth smiling through blood-red pearly lipstick. The smell of her cheap perfume accosted his senses as she sat herself down, uninvited, opposite him, on the other side of his desk, facing him.

'I want your help,' she whispered.

'What do you mean?'

'I know your secret,' she said.

'What are you talking about?'

'My sister works in the Oxfam shop,' she said in explanation.

Daniel was startled.

'Keep your voice down,' he said, even though the office was empty.

'I'm going to do something illegal, and you're going to help me,' she said.

'What if I don't?'

'I'll tell everybody,' she replied and added cruelly 'No skin off my nose.'

Yippee, thought Daniel, *Excellent!* He battled to keep calm.

In his mind's eye he saw this woman as Fragrant Flower, his arch rival, evil incarnate. The time, his time, was come at last. He felt it in his elegant bones.

The clock showed 12:07 hrs.

'Would you like to join me for a tuna salad baguette?' he asked.

How to make Spaghetti Bolognese

We'd argued again.

The way things were going I should really have said 'We'd argued again, **of course**', and although we were in a strange city we'd turned our backs on each other and stormed off in different directions. It happens!

We each had our own key to the small, airless Italian hotel room I'd booked online so it didn't seem to me like a big deal. I could wander around until my temper cooled and then go back there, drink cheap wine, and wait for Her Majesty to appear.

The argument had been on a reoccurring theme. I keep a journal. There, I admit it, what's wrong with that?

'You're always scribbling away in that bloody journal. Why don't you just enjoy the moment, without having to write everything down all the time?', or 'You think more of that bloody journal than you do of me!', were just some of the accusations she'd hurled in my direction. I jotted them down for posterity.

There are worse hobbies or 'obsessions', as she would have it. To me it was a pretty interesting and harmless way of capturing experiences in the moment. Memory is so fallible and here was a way of developing your own personal reference library, a record of your own life, as it happened.

'Do you remember where we were last May 24th?'

'What colour were those flowers on ...?', 'Did we try the lobster in ...?', are all the types of questions that can lead to disagreement and fevered feats of partial remembrance that can disturb a person's sleep for days - or should I say nights? And here was the solution. Just say 'Please wait a moment', turn to the bookshelf, pick the right volume, turn to the right page and 'Voila!', question answered, problem solved, the facts of our lives laid bare for reference.

You'd think she'd thank me but no ... oh no.

I slowed my pace and turned my head to confirm that I had now lost sight of Her. There were people milling across my eye line so I held the pose a moment or two just to be sure. I was sure.

So now I had some time to kill. I made a note of my predicament and listed the options. It was when I wrote 'eat' that I reached my decision. Arguing builds an appetite and, I noted, it was already 15.07 hrs (Local Time) and lunch had been overlooked.

I now had a mission, a purpose, and scrutinised each menu I came across, set on easels or pasted in windows to entice custom. I glanced surreptitiously at other people's half-eaten plates of food, dripping in a rainbow variety of sauces, as satisfying to the eye as to the appetite.

To help me choose a suitable venue I made a short list of requirements,

1. Must be local Italian food - no burgers, no spaghetti with chips!

2. I would prefer my own table in a cool, shaded spot (I have sensitive skin).

3. Not too many other people - the noise, the fuss ... Yeugh.

4. Not cheap-cheap but not rip-off-the-tourists prices either.

I didn't think that this would be too difficult a list to satisfy but after a full 46 minutes 37 seconds of fruitless searching I was beginning to despair.

That's when I saw the blackboard, chalked in English,

"Fresh homemade Italian Food

Meal deal of the Day

Spaghetti Bolognese + Glass local Red"

Underneath was a thickly marked arrow. It pointed down some stone steps that themselves disappeared into a narrow, dark passageway.

Relieved and determined to eat, even if only 3 of my 4 criteria could be met, I made a note of the price and walked down into the coolness.

As my eyes became accustomed to the more forgiving diffuse light I saw an open white wooden door and another arrow pointing inwards with the word "Restaurant" helpfully added.

Ducking below the lintel I entered. Looking around I found that I was in a pleasingly small dining room containing six or seven tables that were covered in white tablecloths and provided with rustic wooden seats. There was only one other family present, sitting around the longest table, eating quietly.

After the glaring al fresco dining of the busy streets above it was like entering a cave, full of coolness and calm.

Bare bulbs cast a yellow light across the room, casting shadows. Through an open doorway in the far wall flickered a brighter light, obscured by the shape that came through it and now walked towards me.

He was a big man. In all directions he was a big man, making the restaurant seem even smaller. Although his face was in shadow I could see his smile, the shining white of perfect teeth.

'Welcome to my restaurant,' he said, in impeccable English.

'You know I'm English?' I asked.

His smile broadened.

'A lucky guess, after so many years ...' he shrugged his shoulders, 'Let me show you to a table, are you alone?'

I reluctantly said that I was.

She would have liked this place. She didn't know what She was missing.

The table was neat and tidy, the tablecloth real linen, and clean. I sat as much in the light as possible so that I could see what I was writing.

'What can I get you?'

'The Meal of the Day,' I said, 'and could you tell me about the wine.'

'A good choice,' he beamed, 'our speciality. I can guarantee that you will not have tasted anything quite like it,' he paused, glancing back at the door through which he'd entered, it must have lead to the kitchen, 'My wife is an incredible woman,' he said, 'she makes the food from the heart, from the soul. Her sauces, aah, her sauces, they are to die for. I am such a lucky man to have a wife like this.'

A far-away look came into his eye. This level of unsolicited praise was very different to the current state of play in my own relationship. I needed to bring him back down to earth.

'And the wine?' I asked, stony faced.

'Ooh the wine,' he replied, opening his arms wide in an all-embracing gesture of appreciation, 'a floral, cherry red, deep in flavour to complement the food, produced from our traditionally rich and fertile soils, the vineyard not more than 30 kilometres from this very spot, the perfect accompaniment.'

'OK,' I said sceptically, 'Thanks. Sounds good.'

For the price, the food and the wine could not possibly be as good as the picture he was painting. He was a good salesman, perhaps over-selling to ensure I stayed in his mostly empty establishment. However I was so hungry that it could all have come from a tin as far as I was concerned. I would still have been happy.

By the time my food arrived the other family of diners had finished their meal, paid the bill and left amidst a hail of 'Grazies', 'Pregos', and 'Arrivedercis' whatever that meant - Languages is not my strong suit.

I was now the sole remaining customer. I made a note.

The Spaghetti Bolognese, together with a small basket of fresh bread, was placed in front of me with a flourish. Steamingly heaped on a large plate it begged to be eaten. Taking a small step backwards the big man uncorked a bottle of red wine, filled a large glass to a generous level and pushed it towards me.

'Although we call the dish Spaghetti Bolognese to avoid confusion,' he said, 'the pasta is in fact tagliatelle. It is more traditional here in Italy and so much better for this particular dish. Enjoy!'

The aromas that floated up to meet my drooling senses were superb. Rich in meaty goodness balanced with tomato, basil, onion and topped with a sprinkling of Parmesan.

I carefully wrapped strands of the tagliatelle around my fork. A mix of the other ingredients magically fastened themselves to the pliant pasta strips. I took a mouthful.

Oh my god!

Oh ... my ... god!

Never had I tasted anything so good. I made only the quickest of notes in my journal before losing myself in the food. The smells, the flavours, the textures, all beautifully matched by the subtlety of the wine that was both sharp enough to cut through the richness of the food and yet not too sharp so as to overpower it.

If food can elevate the soul, my soul was elevating.

It was as I was wiping the plate clean with the freshest of fresh bread that my host reappeared.

'You like?'

Like? Like! I struggled to keep calm. I had yet to pay the bill and could not believe that the price listed was correct. I was happy to pay more but did not want to show my hand too soon.

'Very nice,' I said, not wanting to make a public show of my true exuberance.

She would have loved this, I thought, ha-ha just wait until I tell Her all about it.

The big man turned and called a name that I didn't quite catch. Within a few seconds a beautiful dark haired woman appeared at his side. He said something to her in Italian. She replied and then smiled at me and nodded.

'My wife is pleased that you like her food.'

'May I ask about the recipe?'

He turned to his wife and there followed a short conversation which was interrupted by a knocking at the restaurant door.

I looked across, surprised. In my distracted state I had not noticed that the door had been closed, the chalked signs moved inside.

The big man moved swiftly to the door, unlocked it and opened it an inch or two, 'Il ristorante e chiuso,' he said brusquely, 'Chiuso!'

He closed and relocked the door. I heard feet receding outside.

'I am so sorry,' he said returning to my table, 'now where were we, ah yes, the recipe, I'm sure you will understand that this is a family secret but my wife is willing to admit that it contains garlic, cloves, celery and bay leaves,' he paused, 'but it is the meat that gives it that special, I am sure I am not exaggerating when I say, unique taste. The meat is both lean and juicy and adds delicate flavours to the sauce.'

I imagined I could still taste it - delicious.

'I would love to eat here again,' I said, 'and bring along my partner this time. I'm sure she would love it.'

The big man turned to his wife and they talked for a few moments, becoming increasingly animated. I was not sure what I had said to produce this change.

Eventually, his demeanour less cordial, he said, 'My wife tells me that unfortunately this will not be possible.'

She smiled apologetically.

'Are you closing down?' I asked.

'No, it's not that.'

'Taking a holiday?'

'No.'

I'd run out of ideas.

'Ah, well. Never mind. I'll tell Her all about it anyway. Explain what She's missed. Her fault, not mine.'

'It's because we've run out of meat,' said the big man lowering his head, 'I'm so sorry.'

This was said with such emotion that it surprised me, and when he raised his head I was sure I could see tears forming in his eyes. Here was a man who took his business to heart.

'It's OK,' I said, trying to lift the mood, 'don't worry about it.'

And in demonstration of my lack of concern I made a quick note in my journal, put it in my pocket and pushed back my seat from the table in preparation for my departure.

'What are you doing?'

Although a strange question I thought that I must have unintentionally been impolite in some way. After such a meal impoliteness on my part was definitely not justified and I thought that perhaps my error had been in omitting to request the bill. To rectify this slight I resolved to pay whatever was asked (plus a small tip) and looked forward to getting back outside and into the sunshine.

'I'm sorry,' I said, 'how rude of me. How much do I owe you?'

The man turned imploringly to his wife. She shook her head.

'Nothing,' he said and I saw one of his big hands clench and...

...and that was the last thing I remember before waking up in here with a sore head and the sound of my own pulse throbbing in my ears.

...I don't know how long I've been here. I don't actually know where 'here' is other than noting that it's a small dark room with a single vertical slit for a window that lets in a small, but nonetheless welcome, amount of light and air. I've tried calling but without reply. At least I've still got my journal and can update the entries...

...The big man has just talked to me. He's explained the situation. I don't have long left...

...I spent the night crying. I'm going to push my journal through the slit. Even if I die I want someone to find it and know what happened to me, to stop it happening again, to make these people pay...

Why me I keep asking myself ... Why me ... Why?

... I'm writing this before they come for me. At least my journal will see daylight again. I can only hope that it's found.

I can hear footsteps on stone, a key in the lock, the rasping of metal on metal.

Oh my god this is it.

All I really want to say is ...

****

In the little-frequented back alley the man picked up the book. Opened it and looked at the words. The writing was generally rounded and clear. However as he could not understand English it didn't mean anything to him.

Thinking it may be of some small value to someone else he tucked it into his shirt before returning to sift through the other garbage that lay about, hoping to find something to eat.

Although his clothes were ragged you could see that he was doing his best to keep himself clean and tidy. Painfully thin he was still a proud man, willing to work hard and for long hours. He just needed somebody to give him a break.

Lost in his own thoughts, ferreting for food, he didn't hear the door open, didn't see the big man as he took in the scene, using his hand to shade his eyes from the lowering sun, calling to him in guttural Italian.

When the thin man finally registered that the sound was directed at him he looked up, expecting to be abused, to be told to move on. But the big man was smiling and waving to him, inviting him in. Perhaps this was the break he had been hoping for, perhaps this was a chance to make a friend.

He smiled back and moved towards the open door.

Two rooms

Families are such strange things, always unique and usually dysfunctional. It is always best to stay clear of family disputes and never get between bears and their cubs. But then again I'm not very good at following my own advice.

The dispute in question was between a 20 year-old tearaway called Paulo, a spoilt brat from a rich and disreputable family, and a rival mobster's daughter called Marietta that Paulo had managed to get pregnant.

In a conciliatory gesture the girl's father, Franco, had set fire to the boy's purple Maserati and in retaliation the boy's father, Xavier, had sunk Franco's favourite power boat. The tit for tat was showing all the signs of unstoppable escalation without any prospect of resolution whilst at the same time the girl's predicament continued to grow. In desperation the fathers decided that the best thing to do was to find somebody else to blame.

This was where I came in.

My brief was quite simple and improbable. I had to somehow settle the dispute to the satisfaction of all parties. I talked to both fathers to understand where they were coming from.

Xavier wanted me to help him make Franco see that 'boys will be boys' and that if his daughter was a slut that wasn't Paulo's fault.

Franco told me he just wanted the boy and didn't mind in how many pieces.

From the outset I was smart enough to realise that these contradictory negotiating outcomes were not conducive to compromise but I owed somebody a favour – and it had been called in. Given the choice between the devil and the deep blue sea I chose the devil.

A 19th century stone built guesthouse, formally the family home of Victorian industrialists, had been taken over for the purposes of the arbitration. It still retained many period features and was approached along a winding gravel drive bordered with lawns.

Our assigned meeting rooms were named after significant battles of the Napoleonic wars.

Being a negotiator-for-hire is not easy, at the drop of a hat you have to pull on a mask of social affability and pretend to be fascinated by your paying client's problems. In this case pulling on the mask had been a particularly arduous task. I'd had a very long and a very frustrating morning assiduously passing back and forth between the two intransigent parties, neither used nor willing to compromise. A resolution was looking extremely unlikely and I was beginning to think of ways of extricating myself from this mess unharmed – or as unharmed as possible.

The state of play, reached by my best endeavours at shuttle diplomacy, was that Xavier was willing to offer €500,000 as a form of compensation as long as Franco would then forget about the matter. He didn't care what happened to the girl, or the baby. Franco on the other hand was offering €750,000 as a form of dowry and very badly wanted some personal time with Paulo.

Xavier's party occupied the large "Austerlitz" meeting room on the ground floor of the building. From the ceiling hung a plastic candelabra comprising six egg shaped electric bulbs on six white plastic faux waxen storks, a strange combination of tackiness coupled with a fleeting reference to opulent grandeur. A long table ran down the spine of the room surrounded by red leather seats without arms. Jugs of water, fruit juices and glasses were distributed untouched along the tabletop. In one corner was a bar, well-stocked with whiskey and gin, the bottles now half empty. The wall opposite the door was taken up by a large bay window which overlooked the gardens.

By this time in the afternoon I almost needed a machete to slice my way wearily through the fug and slide my behind unwillingly back on a well-worn seat adjacent to the long, polished, Victorian oblong surface. I scraped the mahogany legs of the chair on the parquet floor as I settled down, letting everybody know I was there.

On the other side of the table sat Xavier, a thickset man with black slicked hair and a worn face. He didn't look happy. On either side of him sat what I can only describe as thugs. They had said nothing throughout the whole morning but did a mean job of making me feel increasingly uncomfortable. Further down the table and towards the bay window sat Xavier's wife Julietta, a large busted unnaturally blonde woman, and the boy himself, Paulo.

'He is willing to increase his offer to €800,000,' I said, 'your offer of compensation remains rejected on principle.'

Julietta was the first to respond. She spoke to her husband,

'Xav, we cannot give our son to Franco. You know what he will do.'

Xavier did not look at his wife but instead he glared at me as if all this was my fault.

'We're getting nowhere,' he said.

It sounded like a threat.

'But dad…' began Paulo.

'Shut up,' interrupted Xavier, 'this has nothing to do with you.'

Au contraire, I thought. It has everything to do with him.

'I think…,' Paulo persisted, but his father cut him off.

'You are not here to think,' he said, his voice raised, his fists clenched, 'you are the future of this family and I am here to protect that future.'

The boy sighed.

The father grated his teeth. You didn't have to be a genius to know he'd known happier times.

Turning to me he said, 'You're the expert. What do we do now?'

At the end of the day negotiations are about people, competing parties seeking a win or at worst a no-lose outcome.

'Are we at least sure that Paulo is responsible?' I asked.

'Yes,' blurted out Paulo before his father could stop him, 'and I want to…'

'Never will a son of mine associate himself with the Franco family,' snarled

Xavier, 'It is many generations now that we have feuded, and with good reason!'

'It's just that we can no longer remember the reason. Isn't that right Papa? It has been so long that we now hate cach other as naturally as we breathe. But Marietta is not to be hated.'

'Sssssh,' whispered his mother putting her arm around his shoulders. He shrugged her off, got up and started to pace around anxiously.

'Would you like to increase your offer of compensation?' I asked desperately seeking a next move, however futile it might be.

'Yes, yes offer them a million,' said Xavier throwing up his arms, 'but you must get me an alternative to releasing my son into their dirty hands.'

It was worth a try. At least it gave me a little breathing space to think of something that could possibly break the deadlock.

As I was getting up to leave Paulo approached and bent down, seeming to pick something up from under the table, close to my feet.

'You seem to have dropped this,' he said, handing me a smartphone.

I had not dropped my phone, and even if I had this one wasn't mine.

I took it, like a drowning man clutches at straws.

'Thanks,' I said, 'clumsy of me.'

'No problemo,' he replied, 'I just hope you didn't miss any important messages.'

His father hissed at me and one of his goons shook his head disparagingly. This apparent act of carelessness had done nothing for my street cred.

Between rooms I took a few minutes. Call me perceptive but I wondered ...

I opened up the phone. Helpfully it had no password protection. I scrolled through the messages that Paulo had left for me and then went onto the internet, downloaded a few things and popped around to Reception to organise printouts.

Franco's party occupied an equally sized room on the first floor. This "Waterloo" room contained an oval table, surrounded by high backed hard seats. Refreshments in the form of tea, coffee, beers, biscuits, and crisps were provided and a large but plain window overlooked the car park and beyond to the long gravelled drive. The window was left perpetually open to let in some fresh air.

Re-entering the room I was very conscious that I had nothing very positive to say. Franco nodded to me. He was a broad brute of a man. With the exception of the top of his head he was hairy, black eyes peering from beneath an overgrowth of eyebrows, his chin hidden by an altogether too-black beard for his age. Menacing would be an understatement.

It was almost impossible to imagine that the blonde, petite but blossoming girl that sat not 10 feet away from him was his daughter, although that was a thought that was definitely not worth developing.

Alongside Franco sat a sharp suited individual in glasses, a legal or financial adviser, or both. Franco's wife, Theresa, stood at the window her back towards us, her shoulders shaking slightly.

I nodded back to Franco and sat down. I looked at the large glass curvaceous jugs of water provided. The condensation on the outer surfaces stood proud, sporadically congealing and trickling down like tears, reflecting my mood. Reaching slowly across I poured myself a glass and took a sip. When you've got nothing to say you may as well say it slowly. Franco grimaced.

'Well?' he rasped.

'Well,' I said, tapping the half-filled glass that sat in front of me with my Schaefer pen. Was it half full or half empty I wondered. Just like in the rest of my life I could never tell.

'Gentlemen and ladies,' I said, 'I have talked at length with the Xavier family and hope that you too have had sufficient time to reconsider your position. In order to reach a resolution it is, in my experience, necessary to identify and consider possible areas of compromise.'

Franco waved his hand in the direction of his daughter, 'Marietta is pregnant. There is no compromise in that. She is not half pregnant. Paulo is the father. There is no dispute on that. He is not half the father, or 80% the father, or 30% the father. Where,' he said pushing his head forward, his complexion reddening with anger and frustration, 'where is there the room for compromise?'

He had a good point but I had to keep the dialogue going for at least one more round. I stayed silent.

Franco shrugged his solid looking shoulders. His bald head glistened with sweat and he took a white linen handkerchief from his pocket and used it to wipe his face, head and hands.

'What more do you want from us?' he said, in an almost conciliatory tone, 'We know the boy is responsible and we want him. We are offering a substantial dowry to avoid a vendetta.'

'Very generous,' I said, with what I hoped was a winning smile, 'but as you know there is a feeling that it is not so much a marriage but more of a funeral that is being proposed,' I paused, 'and this view appears to be unshakeable.'

The beads of sweat that reappeared on the frowning forehead indicated that this belief was not too wide of the mark.

'Father!' shouted Marietta, 'please don't hurt him. You know that I...'

He cut across her words, banging his large gnarled hand on the table.

'You know my opinion,' he said.

'You know what I want to do,' his daughter persisted.

'Yes, but this is between Xavier and me. We go back a long way,' countered her father brisling, 'Of all the boys, in all world ...,' he trailed off, exasperated.

I'd put the phone on the table in front of me, on silent, and noticed the arrival of a new message. I read it,

Gents toilets ground floor now P

Who could turn down such an attractive invitation?

'Let me have one more try,' I said, desperate just to get out of the room.

'One more,' he said, 'and please try hard, try very hard. I don't like people who let me down.'

My day just continued to get better, I thought.

As I passed by Reception I picked up my printouts.

'Congratulations,' smiled the young, blonde, be-suited receptionist.

'Thanks,' I said, my smile less genuine.

My first impression of Paulo had been that he was an idiot and although he was proving himself to be somewhat tech savvy he hadn't done anything to alter that opinion. I didn't like him. I didn't like what he stood for. I didn't like what he did. All that said, if helping him could get me out of this mess then I was all ears.

I pushed through the door marked "Gents" and found him there, leaning against the sinks, smoking.

'So what's the plan?' I said without preamble.

'I'm going to tell them I was attacked,' he said, 'and I've got Marietta's mobile phone number so I'll send her a message. What meeting room are they in?'

I told him, though I wasn't sure I was following his drift.

'So now you just have to hit me,' he said stubbing out his cigarette.

This I could understand and it was too good an invitation to pass up. I moved towards him swiftly, taking him by surprise, turning him around and smashing his face into the wall. With the day I was having it was almost therapeutic.

If there was one thing that Paulo could do well it was bleed.

'That's en...,' he spluttered.

I pretended not to hear and punched him in the stomach, smashing my fist into his gaping mouth as he doubled up.

He slid to the floor groaning.

I left him there.

No need to thank me, I thought.

I meandered slowly back to "Waterloo" allowing as much time as I sensibly could before I re-entered the room.

The normal pleasantries concluded I was just beginning to wonder whether I had hit Paulo too hard when the door was flung open and Xavier charged through, followed closely by his wife and his two minders.

'You bastard!' Xavier shouted, 'You've beaten up my son. I should have known that you're never to be trusted.'

Franco looked at him in genuine surprise.

'What are you talking about you old fool. You always did talk gibberish. I haven't been anywhere near your son, mores the pity. I'd like to have him castrated.'

They moved towards each other. Violence threatened.

'Sit down!' I shouted. I could surprise myself sometimes with my power to command.

The noise stopped, all eyes turned to me. Their attention was so fixed that it would even have been possible for someone to creep from the room unnoticed – if they'd been so inclined.

'Sit,' I repeated more calmly.

They sat. Franco sat beside Theresa, Xavier beside Julietta, the rest of the entourage alongside their respective benefactors.

'I have something to say,' I said, 'that you all need to hear.'

'Then say it,' growled Xavier, 'and then let me tear his ears off.'

'You will lose your eyes first,' snarled Franco.

'Stop,' I said, 'I have something for you.'

Goons, lawyers, wives and fathers, I looked into a sea of eyes waiting expectantly. Now I had to make the most of it.

I produced two pieces of A4 paper and slid one copy towards Xavier and Julietta and one towards Franco and Theresa. I gave them time to take it in and awaited their reaction. I didn't have to wait very long. Franco and Xavier let fly guttural expletives, Julietta and Theresa gazed at one another from opposite sides of the table.

'Yes,' I said, 'copies of a marriage license. Certified and verified.' Not quite true but close enough, 'It therefore appears that no misdeed has been perpetrated. As you can see Paulo and Marietta were married nine months ago.'

Outside a powerful engine roared into life. Someone was being heavy on the accelerator. The two men looked at each other and raced to the window. They were just in time to see a blue Lamborghini convertible, with its roof down, speeding away, wheels spinning, gravel flying. Even from the restricted view of their fast receding backs the identity of the two occupants was unmistakable.

I decided to slip out of the room. I didn't think my presence could add anything more to the proceedings. My job was done. I would live to fight another day and I was pretty sure that the in-laws had some more talking to do.

Surprise, Surprise!

When I read your scribbled card
'Wish you were here
The weather great, the food OK
I miss you very much'

I thought I would surprise you
in your hotel
during your Business trip
and booked a cheap flight

Tired but happy I arrived,
checked my room and
keen to see you ran down to
the blue sparkling pool

And there you were all oiled
and looking fine
Your secretary's fake boobs
heavy in your face

Her fake smile, fake ruby lips
taking you in
leaning over you kissing
your too willing mouth

I should not have lost it but
I was hurting
and followed you to your room
to your big shared bed

And in the quiet that followed
your love making
the gas hissed and you both slept
Bodies intertwined

Memories of how we lay
in times gone by
seared my dry eyes to tears
as I left you to die

Being married to a poet
is not easy
I must think about how to
write your eulogy

Maybe I should start it with
'He knew how to
write but was not always
hot on accuracy.'

The trouble with Catfish*

***Definition of Catfish** – A person who uses a false identity on social media to pursue deceptive online romances.

It is raining.

A young woman stands facing a black door. The rain runs down the door in tears of silver. The woman is around thirty but looks, has dressed to look, younger. Her long blonde hair is tied back, she is slim, her skin is pale, her eyes dark brown, her lips a painted poppy red. She wears a scarlet coat that is dripping rainwater from the hem. A smart shoulder bag hangs down at her hips, the strap is corded and taut from the weight. Her high heel shoes match her lips. Black nylon stockings show between the coat and the shoes, the seams precisely straight.

She shivers then moves to a matrix of buttons that protrude from the wall alongside the door. She hesitates and then reaches out a slim finger and selects 9, presses, and waits.

'Yes.'

It is a male voice, made ageless by the static.

'It's Sarah.'

'Ah, Sarah, I'm so pleased you could make it.'

There is a metallic click as the lock on the door is remotely disengaged.

'I'm on the top floor, there's only the one door so you can't miss it,' then after a slight pause, 'I'll leave it open for you, just walk straight in.'

She pushes the door open and stands on the threshold looking into the darkness of an unlit hallway. She could turn back. This is her last chance to turn back.

She sighs gently to herself and enters.

The plaster walls are peeling and pockmarked with grey. Chunks of fallen plaster litter the floor. There is a layer of dust covering an assortment of accumulated junk; plastic carrier bags, pieces of carpet, empty syringes. In the gloom and musty dampness the young woman picks her way carefully up two flights of bare wooden stairs. Her hard-soled footsteps echo, the sound bouncing off the claustrophobic walls as if she were ascending a bell tower in a church.

On the top floor is a single attic apartment. The ceiling slopes down on either side, exposed wooden joists hover threateningly overhead. It is as if the world is closing in, as if the future has set itself in a single straight unstoppable line.

A fissure of oily yellow light guides her to the door. She sees the tarnished number 9 and bites her lip.

The time for reticence is gone. Her brown eyes glisten in the artificial light as she pushes open the door and steps in.

At first she can hear no sound.

'Hello?'

There is no reply. She follows the light seeking its source and enters a small shabbily furnished room. A beaten up sofa fills one wall. A table and two chairs stand in the centre.

Behind her she hears the apartment door close. A key rasps as the lock slides home. She has made her bed and now she has to lie in it.

She turns.

'Hello, Sarah,' says the man, smiling.

She makes her way to the table, walks around it and sits on one of the chairs. Now she is facing the voice.

The room is full of shadows and from their depths steps a middle-aged man, balding, short, and strong.

Sarah gasps.

'I'm so sorry I'm not twenty one,' he says.

'Oliver?'

'Another lie I'm afraid. But it will do, Olly if you'd like.'

The man moves to the table, pulls back the second chair and sits down opposite Sarah. He smiles. She can smell his peppermint breath.

'You look exactly as you did in your pictures,' he says.

'Your photographs?' stammers Sarah.

'I'm sorry,' he says, 'but I'm pleased you liked my choice.'

'But our online chats ... for hours ... the things you said.'

'Practise,' he says leaning over the table and staring into Sarah's brown eyes, 'I'll do my very best to make this evening as pleasant as possible Sarah, and oh by the way, you didn't tell anybody you were coming here did you?'

Sarah shakes her head.

'Oh, good. May I have your phone.'

Sarah reaches into a coat pocket. The coat is still wet from the rain and drips onto the floor.

She takes out her phone and hands it to him.

The man calling himself Oliver rises from his chair.

'Would you like a drink? Make you feel good. So we can have a nice time.'

He walks to a cupboard, empty except for a bottle and two glasses. He half fills one glass and hands it to Sarah.

'There you are. I want to be nice to you,' he says, smiling.

She takes a drink, feels the raw

sharpness of the cheap alcohol sear her throat. She puts the glass down on the table in front of her.

The rain patters against the roof. Sarah hears her heart beating in her ears. Like the rain, like internal rain.

'Do you get many girls like me?' she asks.

The man is surprised.

'You could unlock the door. You could let me go,' she says.

The man laughs and moves around the table, to Sarah's side of the table, and stands behind her. She tries to get up. Strong hands on her shoulders stop her.

'Now let's start by taking off that coat of yours,' he says.

The man starts to lift the coat from her shoulders.

'I'll do it,' she says.

Sarah rises from her seat, steps away from the chair to give herself space. She turns to face the man and looks at him. The coat drops to the floor, made heavy by the rain.

'You like being in control don't you,' she says.

She strides to the middle of the room. She is wearing a 2-piece gym-suit, tight black with silver threaded seams. The suit ends 6 to 8 inches above the knee giving way, incongruously, to the black nylons, the precisely straight seams and the stark redness of the high-heeled shoes. Clear vinyl surgical gloves cling skin-tight to her hands.

His surprise is palpable.

'Do you remember their names, their faces even?' she asks.

He is impatient now. His teeth are bared as he replies,

'Talking time is over. It's time to play.'

'Do you remember?' she insists.

He comes in close and Sarah strikes. It takes only one punch to the vagus nerve to send him into blackness, suddenly and without warning. She watches as his body crumples to the floor.

His consciousness returns wrapped in pain. He opens his eyes. His mouth is taped and he is standing on one of the chairs. There is a noose around his neck. The cord is looped around one of the exposed joists, it is taut. His hands are tied behind him.

She has taken off the black nylons and the high-heeled shoes and is now wearing white trainers. She removes the tape from his mouth.

He spits at her but misses.

She waits for him to grasp the new situation. She has time, plenty of time.

'Do you feel the noose, the fibres rubbing against your skin? Let me loosen it for you. Talk to me, how are you feeling?' she says.

His eyes give away his fright. The loosened rope gives him voice.

'You bitch,' he snarls.

'Oh come on, you can do better than that. Do you enjoy the chase?'

She loosens the rope a little further.

'It takes time. You've got to be careful, gentle, and playful. Each fish takes a different bait,' he says.

'And you're a good fisherman aren't you.'

'I've learnt through trial and error. Young girls love flattery. Love to be loved.'

‘And that's how I found you,’ she says.

He stops.

‘What?’

‘Everybody has their own footprint, they taught me that in the Army, a certain way of doing things. No matter how many different identities you go through you can’t hide your uniqueness of character, the traits that give you away.’

There is silence and then he attempts to smile. He is proud of his technique.

'What is your real name?' she asks.

He shakes his head so vigorously that the chair rocks. He gasps, struggles and regains his balance.

‘“Oliver” it is then. I don't mind. You see I'm not really called “Sarah” either. We're both Catfish swimming in the same pool you and me. Do you think it's big enough for both of us?'

His desperation is increasing, but he feels there is hope. She doesn't look, or act, like a murderer.

'Well “Oliver” let me tell you what happens when your girls go home. They're at best traumatized, can't sleep, suffer depression, can't tell anyone what's happened to them. They feel humiliated, or used, or worthless, they may even contemplate suicide. Do you ever think about that?'

His face hardens.

'It's not my fault what happens afterwards. It's their fault. Everyone's got choices,' he says.

He steadies himself and looks straight into the young woman's eyes.

'Why are you teasing me if you're just going to hang me? Let's end this game. You win. Let me down. You've had your fun.'

'And then ...?'

Silence.

'You see "Oliver" my problem is that even if you begged for your life, even if you promised to change, we both know that you wouldn't.'

'You're not a murderer.' It is a statement not a question.

For the first time she is unsure.

He senses that this is his chance.

'Let me go now. Let's both go home. No hard feelings,' he says.

'On active service,' she says, 'you get used to death. It's different from justice. There's no justice in war, just luck and training.'

She hesitates.

'Let me go.'

'OK,' she says, 'that's enough.'

Relief floods through him. He starts to think ahead, about how he will tackle this bitch when he's free. She took him by surprise but now his turn is coming.

The young woman starts to move. She walks behind him and unties his hands.

She kicks away the chair.

'Wha...,' his lips curl as he begins to choke.

She watches him struggle.

She knows it won't take long and reaches into her shoulder bag to take out a photograph. She holds it in front of his staring eyes.

'Do you remember her?'

He is a fit man. His movements are strong and muscular. His hands grasp at his own neck, tearing at the cord. She fears he will free himself. But his height and weight are against him. There is too great a distance between joist and head, feet and floor, arms and walls.

She watches.

'That was my sister,' she says.

His colour changes, pink to blue, blue to blue-black.

She picks up her scarlet coat. It is reassuringly cool in its dampness as she slips her arms through the sleeves. She picks up her bag, cordless now, but heavy with tape and shoes. Then she retrieves her phone and the key to the apartment from the man's sagging pockets. She unlocks the door, leaves the key in place and walks slowly down the dark stairs. There is no need to rush.

Now at home she sits in front of a blazing coal fire, in her head she hears the words of her therapist, 'It can help to write things down, just for yourself, putting things on paper can help you sort through …'.

She moves slowly and calmly across the carpeted floor and sits at a small desk that ripples in the flickering shadows from the fire. She picks up a pen and starts to write,

Dear Sis,

I'm sorry I wasn't there for you when you needed me. I got the message out in Iraq, only a week before I was due to come home. Surrounded by death your death devastated me. I'm sorry you couldn't talk to anyone. Mum said she didn't see it coming, that it was just like any other day when she came home to find you hanging there. You looked so lonely she said. She took you down, cradled you in her arms and cried before she called anyone.

Your internet history gave me the leads.

He'll not do it again.

Mum and I will be OK. I just want you to know that. We'll miss you every day but we'll find a way. It's hard.

All my love,

Your big Sister

She stares at what she has written, picks up the paper, scrunches it into a ball and walks over to the fire. She throws the letter into the flames and watches it as it shrivels, curls and blackens, and then flares into yellow-red tendrils that disappear up into the redeeming blackness of the chimney.

Then she stretches, her muscles tight but loosening, and goes to the bottom of the hall stairs. She looks up upwards and calls,

'Mum, I'm back. Shall I put the kettle on?'

Starting out

He closed his eyes so that he could see the boy more clearly.

Just as the eye completes a picture that is not complete so the mind seeks to complete a memory.

It was a warm summer afternoon in the valley. Wild flowers lifted their showy heads above the green blanket and nodded in yellows and reds and blues. The red poppies rose highest, their black hearts beating to the rhythm of their single day in the sun.

By a chuckling stream Jack Alexander Steele stood to attention, his raggedy trousers, cut off below the knees, covered the tops of woollen socks that went on to bury themselves in laced, scraped, hop-nailed boots. There was a broad smile on his face as, oblivious to the real world that surrounded him, his eyes gazed into the depths of a conjured landscape.

He held a half-rotten branch tightly in both of his small hands. It was bigger than he was. To Jack though it was not a branch, it was a Martini Henry rifle, breech-loading and rifle bored, the pride and joy of any old soldier. He stroked the stock, he knew from his grandad that real soldiers loved their rifle, fed and cleaned it with the care a mother would lavish on a firstborn.

This rifle, Jack's rifle, had been well-used over the last blue-sky hour and the barrel was scorching hot from the fight. Jack lifted the loaded gun to his shoulder, a familiar, smooth, movement that his grandad had taught him as they relived together the old man's war stories, the African heat, the dust caking the back of their throats, the red coat uniform essential so that if they were wounded the blood would not show. All the time his grandad, pipe held between his teeth, talked of these olden days Jack would stare at the scars on the old man's arm, the badge of a soldier, the sign of a man. Sometimes the old man would let Jack run his fingers slowly along the hairless ridges, feeling the slick unevenness, careful not to hurt. Through the stories they would fight together the unseen hoards until Mary, his mother, called them in to tea complaining that her father was filling Jack's head 'with all kinds of rubbish'.

Jack had learnt his lessons well, he had fought on despite the Sun's searing heat cascading over his light, khaki- coloured helmet and burning the back of his neck a painful red. But he had ignored the pain and earned his "redneck" status. In front of him the black bodies of Zulu warriors were piled high, some still moaning and groaning in their death throes.

The onslaught of the ruthless Zulu Impi had been repulsed by the fearless stand of Jack and his imaginary friend, Rupert, who had passed him his ammunition and mopped the sweat from his fevered brow. But it had been achieved only by the skin of Jack's red-coated teeth. Now that it was over and the fight had been won he stood erect, shoulders back, chest out, his face set serious in a look of grim pride and superiority as he muttered to himself and to the world in general, 'For Queen, for country, and for the Empire!'.

'Jack, what the hell are you doing?'

Jack turned towards the call. It was Edward, his elder brother, and it broke the spell. The soldier's pith helmet of tea-stained tan dissolved into a head of matted, tousled fair hair encased in a flat cap. The soldier's coat, red threaded beneath a brown covering of African dust, melted back into a dirty slate grey jacket, waistcoat and off-white flannel shirt that was the more usual uniform of the colliery community of which Jack was a small part.

Edward, larger and more powerful than Jack by grace of his extra years was shouting to him,

'Our Mam has sent me to look for you. She's worried sick about her little favourite as usual. I've been bloody looking all over the bloody place for you.'

Mary did not allow swearing in the house so Edward, old enough to be working down the pit and drinking with the local men, made up for it when he was out of her earshot.

Jack stared at him from the far bank of the stone-chattering, clear flowing stream. Between the brothers and across the stream lay a conveniently fallen tree trunk, struck by lightning in some earlier forgotten storm, and now used by the local boys as a convenient crossing.

But Jack would not be tethered to reality so easily. His fertile imagination worked a new scene. In clothes of lincoln green he turned to face his brother, his back stretched to the very limits of his 10-year-old tallness.

'Do not attempt to cross Little John for I, Robin Hood, am your superior and have right of passage.'

'What the fuck....?'

Taken off-guard Edward hesitated, then grinned.

His younger brother's imagination never ceased to amaze him and looking quickly around to ensure they were alone, he rubbed his grimy coal dust black chin, felt the reassuring rasp of unshaven stubble, and decided it would be fun to go along with this newest bout of craziness. Picking up a large stick, a foot or more longer than Jack's, he turned his flat cap peak-to-back, something he always did when he was about to take action, and stepped forward.

'I challenge you Robin Hood,' he shouted, 'for no-one is superior to me. I am Little John, the toughest guy around here.'

'So we must fight,' shouted back Jack, a white smile splitting his soiled features, 'This is war, and our war is our duel.'

Under the cloudless blue summer sky Edward and Jack stepped to the opposite ends of the tree trunk bridge. The chattering stream and the occasional twittering woodland bird bore witness to the approaching conflict.

The bridge was part blackened, carbon-charred from its violent past, and was slowly decomposing. The surface was streaked in browns, yellows and greens, slimy with the encroaching moss and lichen. Bracts stood from its sides like ears, listening but not hearing.

'Come on then Jack, let's be having you,' cried Edward, stepping onto the fallen tree.

'I know not this Jack of whom you speak,' shouted Jack, 'Make way Little John, make way for Robin Hood.'

Jack's words flew from his young clean lungs, clear and boy-pitched, the sound flying through the still, clear, Sunday morning air of childhood. He stepped forward boldly,

'You must be bloody joking,' snarled Edward as he swung his staff in a wide, experimental, aggressive arc, the stream below sighing to the swish of his first haymaker of a blow.

In the story that Jack had heard Robin Hood and Little John duelled to an exhausted standstill. In this more real world encounter however Edward's stick caught Jack "smack" on the side of the head and sent him flailing from the log. Jack's staff somersaulted from his grasp and he scrabbled desperately for a hold but found nothing but fresh air. His world operated in slow motion and he felt like an observer to his own useless efforts.

Spiralling lazily out of control he reached out, stretching, falling agonisingly short of balance or of a safe hold, something, anything that could halt, or at least slow, his decent. But it was not to be and as time fast-forwarded to normal speed he crashed heavily into the cold water of the stream.

Briefly he felt a sharp, knife-like pain accompanied by a reverberating clunk as his head hit a subsurface rock, then his own blackness rose and enveloped him. Slowly a thin red smear unfolded onto the surface of the cleansing coolness of the stream and wound its way downstream.

Edward laughed in his triumph.

'Take that Robin Hood. It was too easy,' he said, adrenaline still pumping through his victorious veins.

He looked down at Jack lying prostrate in the stream and was sure that he was acting, trying some new trick or drama to dilute Edward's conquest.

'Get up!" he called. But Jack did not move.

'Come on, get bloody up,' but there was still no movement, 'Jack stop messing about, I beat you fair and square.'

Met with only stillness and silence, two attributes foreign to Jack's nature, Edward peered more closely and saw the greasy red smear.

Victory turned into panic. He threw aside the now-offending weapon and jumped into the stream. It was only ankle deep and he grabbed at Jack, pulling his face from the water, and shook him back to a dazed semi-consciousness.

'Shit, shit, shit! What will Mam say now ... don't you bloody die she'll kill me ... and what will Dad do?'

Blurred images and muffled sounds, as if half smothered in a blanket, were all that were discernible to Jack and he groaned.

'Oh thank god, thank god! At least you're not dead yet.'

As he began to emerge from his warm, comfortable, pain-free blackness Jack felt an excruciating pain pounding in his head, like the tearing of electrically charged strips from his brain. He moaned and Edward put his arm around his shoulders and dragged him from the water.

'Listen Jack, just tell Mam you fell over, OK? You fell over. Got it. OK?'

Taking the weight Edward half-carried, half-dragged Jack back to the rows of colliery houses that brooded in rows and smoking chimneys, smelling of coal fires.

In the pit village everyone knew everyone else and everyone else's business and as they approached the corner of Cobden Terrace, with number 62 as their destination, the two boys were spotted by a young girl. Anne Hudson was about Jack's age and was skipping and chanting, throwing up dust from the dirt road. She called over,

'What's up Jack, you playing wounded soldiers? Can I be nurse?'

'It's not a game Annie,' Edward shouted back, 'run home, tell our Mam Jack's hurt. Hurt for real.'

Her face changed from smiles to serious and Anne turned and started to run. She was no stranger to the realities of accident, injury or even death and she ran as fast as she could. Clattering up to the open door of number 62 she rushed in yelling,

'Come quick, come quick, Jack's hurt!'

The boys' mother, Mary, was at the kitchen sink. Her youngest son, George, was tugging at her apron for support, unsteady on 1-year-old legs.

By the time the boys reached the familiar scrubbed front step Mary was there amidst a small but growing number of interested, curious or concerned neighbours. Mary wiped her hands on her blue checked apron and a neighbour took charge of George, who was trailing in her wake. Edward was already taller than his mother whose wiry frame belied her strength and she pushed him aside to concentrate on Jack's injuries.

'What's happened? Let me look.'

Mary's fingers parted the matted hair, feeling for damage. She saw the deep cut above Jack's right eye from which blood flowed. Jack winced. Edward started to gabble an explanation.

'So he hit his head?' asked his mother.

'It was a game. It can't have hurt. It must have been when he fell in the stream.'

Mary turned her attention to Edward and saw the slick red patch on his shirt, saw the sweat on his forehead, the fear in his eyes.

'But you're bleeding too.'

'No, no, I'm OK, that's Jack's blood. I carried him back most of the way.'

Mary nodded and snapped back to focus solely on Jack.

'So he fell in the stream?' she said over her shoulder as she tried to work out how badly Jack was hurt. He certainly seemed dazed.

'Yes, off that old tree that's there.'

'And he hit his head then?'

'I didn't see,' said Edward, grim-faced, sheepish, holding back.

'OK, stand away now Edward, leave Jack to me. Go and get George and take care of him for me.'

'But...'

Jack blinked and caught a blurred glimpse of his mother's concerned face.

'Jack! Jack! Are you OK pet?'

His head buzzed. He felt the pain, it throbbed like a living thing, with a level of audibility that he thought the whole world must be able to hear. He wanted to escape and reached back for the blackness, warm, welcoming, comforting. The last sounds he heard as he drifted away were in his mother's voice. She was talking to some members of the small crowd that had gathered around.

'Liz can you go get Doctor Pitt. Hannah can you take George off Edward and look after him for a bit. I think we'll be needing some stitches,' and to the rest, 'Doesn't look too bad to me. I can cope with it from here on, thanks.'

Anne Hudson was the last to move away.

A few days later Jack lay on the big couch in the living room opposite the window, sunshine covering and warming him. His grandfather sat alongside in his rocking chair, his face lined and wrinkled with age and as testament to the harsh life he had led. His moustaches, of which he was justly proud, bushed from his upper lip, wiry and rough and still sporting the odd strand of black amongst the grey. Tended and tamed each and every day its condition and fine waxed points were maintained to a military standard. Shirt sleeves folded back to the elbow, the old man smelled perpetually of the tobacco that he used to fill his pipe. His stained fingers, the worn place and yellowing of his teeth gave testament to its frequent use although Mary would have him sit by an open window or go outside whenever she could to 'save the rest of the house from that stink'.

Now he sat in the familiar rocking chair, comfortable in the worn upholstery, softened by use into his unique shape. It was from this chair that he told his stories, some true, some embellished, some complete fantasy, and conjured a world that he and Jack travelled together.

The old man's face was set in concentration as he looked Jack over with watery eyes. Whilst he was doing this the family clock that was the focal point of the room chimed an hour. It was five minutes fast as it always was and the sound disturbed Jack into wakefulness.

As his body moved the shadows cast by the pointed leaves of the aspidistra plant that stood by the window and thrived on neglect, rainwater and cold tea, rippled over him.

'How's it going Jack, how you feeling?'

Jack was still groggy and squinted into the light.

'I'm doing fine grandpa,' he murmured, 'fit as a fiddle and twice as nimble.'

The old man smiled.

'Fit enough for a story?'

Jack rubbed his eyes, yawned, nodded and moved himself into a sitting position. He shook his head to clear it of sleep. The pain from his injury made him wince, but he was now awake.

'What would you like?'

'Anything but Robin Hood,' said Jack, 'I've gone off him.'

The old man looked quizzical, not getting the point.

'OK then,' he said, 'how about a few thousand Zulus?'

'That'll do nicely,' said Jack.

'Well let me just get comfy before we start,' said his grandfather, adjusting the cushions and scraping the rocking chair closer and more into the light that flowed through the window.

As the old man drew nearer Jack could see the scars on his arm, glistening in the sun.

Jack would have a scar of his own now, about an inch and a half long. Right now it was still a swollen ripe red stripe above his right eye sitting atop a blue-black bump, painful to the touch.

'If this is what it takes to get a scar then I don't want any more,' thought Jack as he settled back to listen.

Life and Death

Jack raised a black-smeared hand and looked up through his fingers, protecting his eyes. The circle of daylight grew steadily as the mechanical cage rattled and groaned its way upwards. The crush of human cargo, much to the frustration of the pit management, traveled at a slower regulated speed than when the cage fulfilled its primary purpose of lifting tubs of coal to the surface. There was no profit in lifting men in and out of the ground, the pit's economy was dependent on the number of fully laden lifts of good quality coal that could be got out in a day, every day. The sooner this expensive equipment, capital and running costs calculated and recalculated weekly to the nearest farthing, could return to its proper work, the better.

The whiteness of the men's eyes contrasted starkly with the blackness smeared across their faces and they chattered and joked as they made the familiar journey upwards, shouting to be heard above the clanking of machinery and the voices of others.

Finally the cage broke the surface and came to a grinding stop. A buzzer sounded a safe arrival and wrought iron concertina metal gates were brutally hauled back disgorging the men into the sunlight in a tumbling, mumbling rush, their shoulders stooped, squinting into the unaccustomed brightness, looking only at the ground with a mixture of pain, relief and freedom.

The men fanned out from the pit-head, jostling and colliding with each other in a kind of sleepwalker's gait as their eyes re-accustomed to the light and their pupils shrank to surface-dweller size. Disturbed by the movement tiny flecks of coal dust rose from hair, clothes and skin to float in the air. Caught by the sunlight that had given it birth millennia ago, it glittered, sparkled, swirled and danced round the men, a halo of sharp silver stars, before gently falling to join the other layers of black snow that covered everything, always.

'Thanks fuck that's over,' said Edward turning to Jack and patting him on the back.

As a hewer Edward worked at the coalface. It was damp, dark, and dangerous work with little light from his safety lamp as he sweated to bring out the coal from the seam, being paid by the weight of coal he and his immediate team of four or five managed to get out. His team was also part of a larger team of forty six hewers who worked across the "Baggy" seam in B pit. As the seam was inconsistent in depth and quality of coal the men would rotate positions on a weekly basis to ensure equal opportunity for earnings. On average each man would hew 3.7 tons of coal in each of his seven hour shifts.

Down the pit Edward would strip to his sleeveless rough cotton vest for the work. First he would cut out a layer of coal from the base of the seam swinging his pick in the semidarkness. Always conscious of the dangers of gas, flooding, ceiling collapses and dust explosions, he would curse violently each time the pick unintentionally hit a stone and produced a glittering shower of dangerous sparks that would cascade gaily about him. Having undercut the seam the men would drill into the higher level of the coalface and pack the holes with black powder explosive. A pricker was then inserted and the hole around its stem sealed in with clay. Taking out the pricker then left a hole through to the main powder charge into which a further amount of explosive was inserted packed into a squib. Now was the most dangerous moment of all. The pit face was cleared. The squib was lit and ignited the rest of the powder. It was a dangerous job and many were the stories of near-run-things, accidents, injuries and death. Once the dust had cleared the coal was hacked, broken and shovelled into the tubs that were pulled along their rails by the staunch pit ponies. Then the cycle was repeated, moving steadily through the seam, supporting the ceilings behind you with wooden pit props.

The hewer's job, one of the most dangerous and physical and skilled jobs down the pit was also one of the best paid. There was competition for these jobs and, as a lucky consequence of the pit currently expanding its operations, his undoubted muscular build, and the fact that his father was also a hewer and had used his influence on his son's behalf, Edward had risen into the role quickly. He was proud to be a hewer.

Jack, younger and a more recent recruit to the subterranean world of the pit, was a putter and looked after a number of the pit ponies that pulled the coal tubs to and from the coalface. He loved the job, he loved the ponies. He would talk to them, sometimes even confide some of his secrets to them. He had learnt to know each of them individually, their different personalities and idiosyncrasies. Jack's build was more wiry, less muscular than his elder brother's and his father had not used his influence on Jack's behalf in the same way he had done for Edward. This was the cause of an unspoken bitterness for Jack, evidence of his father's favouring of Edward.

'It's for the best,' his mother would tell him, when he told her how he felt. But he would not and did not listen, believing that it could only be seen one way, his way. He feared and largely respected his father but that didn't mean he had to like him.

Times were good at the pit, a new shaft had been recently sunk and the coal seam was thick and relatively soft. The men were making good money from the tonnage they dug each shift, got into the tubs, into the cage and out, up to the surface, for sorting.

As it was payday Edward and Jack joined the long weekly pay queue and carefully counted and tallied the notes and coins that were handed out to them. The queues contained both underground and surface workers so that it was a fair crowd of people that flowed steadily back to the mining cottage rows in dribs, drabs and groupings.

The houses were owned and built by the pit owners and rented to the mine workers for as long as they earned their keep and not a week longer.

Some of the men went direct and dirty to the village pub, The Barley Mow, the call of the lukewarm beer, darts and dominoes more powerful than that of home or personal hygiene. There was banter and relief and laughter as the men separated naturally into shared-interest groupings. In contrast to the dark working environment underground a number of the men were passionate and competitive in their pursuit of the perfect vegetable from their allotments, the line and speed of their racing dogs, the homing instinct of their home-bred pigeons or the challenge of rabbiting or fishing. Their pastimes were part of their reason to work, something to look forward to, a relief and, for the most obsessed, their real life.

Edward and Jack walked together, making their way home. As always they were discussing their favourite subject, football. Anne Hudson, a surface worker and a sorter of stone from coal, followed a couple of steps behind, listening in.

The zinc bath was already full of hot water when they got home. Steaming in front of the coal fire it sat on the stone fagged floor of their back room that did the whole family for kitchen, washroom, dining room, games room and snug. Their mother smiled at them as they entered through the backyard.

'Take your boots off Edward,' she said, 'and let's get you into this bath before the water goes cold. Jack, don't you bother taking your boots off yet, you can go and fetch some more water and put the kettle and pan on to boil for your bath. I need to be getting on with some cooking if you're to get any tea tonight. Oh, and Jack, keep a lookout for young George while you're out getting the water. He should be getting back from school soon.'

Before Jack and Edward responded to this customary string of instructions they each took their pay out of their pockets and laid it on the table.

'And good afternoon to you to mother,' said Edward as he started to strip off his clothes.

Edward's pale white torso contrasted markedly with the ingrained black of his muscular calves, feet, work-worn hands, arms, neck, face and hair.

Mary took a small notebook, dog-eared from use, and sat at the kitchen table. Carefully counting the boy's pay twice through, to ensure she'd got it right, she added new numbers neatly to the long column of figures.

'I know I'm a bit short this week,' said Edward from the bath, 'but we'll be moving to a softer part of "Baggy" next week so I'll make up.'

Mary nodded and arranged two piles of coins on the table.

'You're money's there when you want it,' she said and rose to lift the lid off a pottery jug, shaped and coloured like a beer barrel, that stood on the corner of the mantelpiece, pushing the rest of the money inside and replacing the notebook behind it.

'Where's granddad?' asked Edward.

'He's up at his allotment, tending to his leeks and his chickens, like they were his babies, probably talking to them most like.'

'Telling them stories about the Zulus,' broke in Jack.

'I thought I told you...' but before she could finish the sentence Jack raised his hands in surrender. His mother smiled. Jack picked up the three empty tin water buckets, turned and walked out through the brick surfaced yard, past the outside solid toilet, out through the wooden planked green painted gate and into the back lane.

On his way to the street's communal water tap Jack saw his younger brother George running home from school, and called over to him.

'Whoa George. Come over here and give us a hand.'

George, who had been slapping his side with the palm of his hand in pretence of riding a galloping horse, stopped dead in his tracks. Plucked from his daydream he looked around to see who had called him. Seeing it was Jack, his face broke into a broad smile, and he galloped his horse to his side.

'And what was school like today?' asked Jack, starting to fill the first of the buckets.

'Brilliant,' said George, who could not stand still and was prancing on the spot, pulling on the reins of his imaginary young stallion, holding it back with difficulty.

'Brilliant? Well that's a new one. What made it so good, was the teacher ill?'

'We did lice,' replied George, 'Did you know that lice have a Latin name,' he paused, 'and I can remember it.'

'Go on then,' said Jack responding to George's enthusiasm, 'You'd better tell me now. You'll of forgotten it by tomorrow.'

'Pediculus humanus capitis,' said George clearly proud of himself, 'hah, and they has no wings and can only live on us humans, sucking our blood.' He made a sucking noise through his teeth.

'Amazing.'

'And that's not all. Their mouths are specially designed to pierce through our scalp,' said George, gnashing his teeth to drive home the point, 'they're only small and they hide in the shadows keeping out of sight, although they make your head itch.'

'Very nice,' said Jack, filling the second bucket and pausing to scratch his head in sympathy with the thought.

'Have you had nits? Dora Heslop's got them. She showed me in the playground. Crawling about they were.'

Jack filled the last of the three buckets and handed one, that was three quarters full, to George.

'I'll get mam to run the nit comb through your hair George and make sure you haven't picked up any unwelcome guests from Dora. Just grab this and let's be getting home. I feel like I'm even more in need of a bath now for some reason.'

They walked back down the street side by side, concentrating, careful not to slop or spill any of the precious water, George's stallion having mysteriously evaporated.

'What would you do if you find any?' asked George.

'Oh, just shave off all your hair and paint your scalp yellow with ointment.'

'Ooooooh,' said George, trying hard to keep his hands away from his hair even though there was an itch that had just started, aching to be scratched. He fell silent and in his mind he saw himself scalped and yellow and in the playground being surrounded by his friends who were pointing and laughing. It was not a pretty thought.

'So why doesn't Dora Heslop have her head shaved and painted yellow?'

Jack thought for a moment,

'She's a girl.'

George couldn't argue with that. Dora Heslop was definitely a girl and girls were definitely different in increasingly mystifying ways.

'I don't think I've got nits,' said George and fell silent, concentrating on carrying the water bucket without spilling any.

It took a long time to get clean and Edward was still soaping and scrubbing when Jack returned with George in tow.

'Howdy George,' said Edward over his shoulder and then shouted, 'Mam, George's back,' up the stairs that lead from the corner of the backroom to the two small bedrooms. There was a muffled reply.

Jack filled the kettle and pans and put them to the fire to heat. Leaning his elbow on the mantelpiece he lit a cigarette.

'Don't ask George what he did at school,' he said to Edward.

'Why what did you do George, you didn't get into trouble again did you? I was always getting into trouble from that Miss Lowther, no wonder she's never got married, bet she's a witch in her spare time.'

George did not rise to the bait, although he would have loved to have swapped stories about Miss Lowther being a witch.

'I don't want to talk about it, I'm going to see if I can help mam,' he said and raced off, his feet clumping as he ran up the wooden stairs.

Jack grinned.

'You shouldn't tease him,' said Edward, 'He might be bigger than you someday and then he'll give you a right good hiding.'

'I'll take my chances.' said Jack, taking the soap and brush and starting to scrub at Edward's back, 'Are you going down the pub tonight?'

'Does a duck quack?' answered Edward.

'Then get out the bath and let me have a turn, the fresh water's boiling now.'

Edward stood up and began towelling himself dry.

'OK, OK, just leave me enough hot water in the kettle for a cup of tea. I thought you might be walking your girl out tonight.'

'What girl's that? I don't have any girl.'

'Jack, you're as blind as a bat if you think that,' said Edward, 'and twice as daft.'

Jack said nothing, only frowned.

As he was getting undressed ready to step into the partially refreshed steaming, soapy water, his grandfather arrived back from the allotment.

'Hi grandpa,' said Jack, 'how's the leeks?'

His grandfather ignored the question.

'I just heerd about them two Tindale boys,' he said, 'Very sad, very sad indeed.'

Jack and Edward glanced at each other but were none the wiser for it.

'We've heard nothing, do you mean the twins?'

'Aye that's right. Been found drowned. Just been round to pay me respects, they've got them laid out in the front room already.'

'What happened?'

'Finish yer bath and then I'll tell the lot of yer together,' said the old man taking four newly laid eggs from his jacket pocket and putting them carefully into a enamelled bowl that was on the kitchen table. 'Helps the laying when I talks to them ya knows.'

Edward had been working down the pit too long for the black on his face and hands to be totally removable, no matter how much soap or how much scrubbing was given to the task. Jack on the other hand was less impregnated and could clean up better. Jack called for his mother who came downstairs and scrubbed his neck, back and behind his ears as she liked to do. Admiring the broad shoulders of her middle son she hoped the pride did not show on her face.

When Jack emerged, Edward and George dragged the bath out through the backyard and poured the dirty water away down the back street gutter, hanging the zinc bath back up on the nail in the outside wall ready to be used again on their father's return in the early morning.

By the time Edward and Jack were dressed in fresh clothes there were mugs of tea waiting on the kitchen table and the family gathered around to hear the news, however shocking.

Grandpa Wallace stroked his moustache, he enjoyed telling stories be they real or imaginary and infused them with a drama, comedy or suspense appropriate to the plot. The real life story of the Tindale twins however could not be anything other than a tragedy.

The Tindales lived in the next row but one and although not well known to the family everyone could remember how the arrival of twin boys as firstborns had been welcomed as auspicious for the whole community and a thing of pride for the lucky parents. It had been a common sight to see the boys rolling around together or getting into trouble for their mischief. They were always arguing but at the same time inseparable.

Gathered together around the kitchen table Grandpa Wallace told his silent, attentive audience that the twins had simply gone off to play after school as they often did. On this occasion they had sneaked off unnoticed, run behind the colliery rows and over to the disused quarry. George butted in to say that it was well known in the playground that there was good pickings of bird's eggs to be found around the quarry and they were probably after them,

'They liked to collect bird's eggs,' he said, 'especially those with coloured spots and splodges.'

Unfortunately, because of the recent heavy rainfall, the quarry, whose sides were steep and relatively bare, was deep with brown, murky water. From what Grandpa Wallace had heard it seemed most likely that one of the twins had climbed a tree which clung to the quarry side and on reaching out to a nest full of birds eggs had simply overbalanced and fallen into the water. His brother instead of running for help had jumped straight in to try and rescue him, even though neither of the two boys were strong swimmers. The slickness and steepness of the quarry wall, the panic which must have set in, the limited strength of the boys and the depth of the water must have all conspired to prevent the boys from hauling themselves out. If they had called for help, which surely they must have done, then the clatter of railway trucks and the distance from the rows had meant their cries had not been heard. Unable to save themselves and exhausted by their efforts they had drowned.

They had been discovered only that morning. The parents had raised the alarm but darkness had hampered the initial search. They were found floating on the surface of the water, face down, hand in hand.

Although death was a constant companion to those who lived in the pit village, disease or accident taking a constant toll, the death of twin boys was particularly poignant.

The old clock chimed in the living room in the silence that followed Grandpa Wallace's explanation.

'So I won't see them at school on Monday,' said George. He understood the attraction of collecting bird's eggs and knew that the school would be quieter without the twins squabbling in lessons and fighting in the playground, but he thought he would still miss them.

'We'll pop in to pay our respects on our way to the Barley Mow,' said Edward.

'That'll be good,' said Mary, 'I'll tell your dad when he gets in from his shift and I'll go round tomorrow. I'll take them some bread and find out when the funeral is.'

Jack and Edward called in at the Tindale's house, taking off their flat caps as they entered. In the far corner of the kitchen were the two corpses, laid out and covered in white sheets. Mrs Tindale, about thirty and heavily pregnant, welcomed them in and directed one of her young daughters to lift the edge of each of the sheets in turn.

'They've laid them out real nice already,' she said, 'and the coffins will be ready tomorrow.'

A younger child, a boy, crawled on the stone-flagged floor and Mrs Tindale gently directed him away from the kitchen fire with her foot.

'We're so sorry,' said Jack, 'If there's anything we can do...'

'Thanks,' said Mrs Tindale, wiping her eye with the corner of her apron, 'Your grandfather has already been round and left us a few eggs.'

They stayed only for a few minutes, remembering the boys together, swapping stories.

'Our mam will come round when she can,' said Edward as they were leaving.

Outside they just looked at each other as they started to make their way to "The Barley Mow".

'Whose round is it tonight?' asked Edward as the lights of the pub rose before them bright and welcoming. They could already hear the boisterous singing and their pace increased.

The light poured out from inside as they approached the threshold and Jack paused to rub his fingers along the scar above his right eye, appearing to suffer intense pain at the touch.

'Alright, I'll buy the first one,' Edward laughed, 'It's a bloody expensive scar that and no mistake.'

Dealing with things

The Barley Mow Inn was always busy, the atmosphere permanently fogged with cigarette and pipe smoke. The background noise rose and fell like waves breaking on a shingle beach, the pulsing chatter punctuated by bursts of laughter and raucous singing that issued from the choir of men that clustered around an old, weather beaten, piano.

This was a place for the men, a men's haven in a man's world. If now and again it was impossible to prevent a person of the female persuasion from crossing the threshold then it was an unwritten but golden rule that she would take her place solely in the small snug that nestled at the back. Here she and her male escort could sit at a table and take a small drink in a civilised manner, maintaining a pretence of deafness to the blasphemous swearing issuing forth from the men in the bar. As most of the men were not allowed to swear in the confines of their own home they made up for it by relaxing their vocabulary in the pub.

The thirst that naturally followed from the exertion expended during a long and sweaty shift underground also gave the men an excuse for a break from their womenfolk and, if the truth be known, the womenfolk a further break from their men, who when at home would be forever demanding food or cups of tea and getting in the way of the endless list of chores that needed doing to keep a pit family afloat.

That the women worked harder than the men would never be admitted. It was the men who brought in the majority of the money to the household and it was their job that kept the roof over the family's head. The women's housework was unpaid and therefore not valued as highly. Their real worth became starkly evident however whenever they weren't there, through illness or childbirth, and all the 'normal' jobs went undone.

With regularly five, six or more children to look after the women ran their own home organisations with military precision. The children were allocated chores, the elder children looked after the younger and the mother controlled the family finances, ensuring that they were stretched to cover food, clothes, cooking, baking, cleaning and that there was even a little left over for the pot.

The doors of the houses were normally open, and never locked. Neighbour knew neighbour intimately and the speed of mouth to mouth communication of news, gossip and rumour was faster than any newspaper could have ever achieved, the details more embellished and, even if they were not always precisely correct, became accepted fact through repetition.

Although the women would generally help each other out with half cups of sugar or flour in lieu of two eggs or half a pint of milk and freely pass on advice, sometimes unwelcome, on the treatment of illness there was also a healthy, although largely unspoken, competition between households. Knowledge and wisdom would be passed from mother to daughter and some of the older women would also choose to mentor younger women whom they particularly liked. At the same time new mothers strove to prove themselves against the tried experience of the older generation. Most of the time this provided a healthy sparkiness but on occasion it would become personal and viciously bitter. Sides would then have to be taken and over time, which could stretch to years, the war would be fought. There could be real casualties.

The men would generally try to ignore these intricate maneuverings and confine themselves to grumbling at the cost of essentials and how little this left over for their beer money.

Parents looked forward to a time when sufficient of their offspring survived to an age when they could bring money of their own into the house. This was the time when luxuries could be afforded but it wouldn't last long before marriage or the lure of a better job somewhere else would cause the youngsters to move out and take on household responsibilities of their own.

The Barley Mow had a regular clientele from the surrounding streets some of whom had their own personal glass or tankard hanging over the bar or held first rights to a particular seat in a corner by the fire. With a flagstone floor, a wooden settle, some benches, a fireplace, and a bar, the place was homely enough and miners who could play the piano were particularly welcome as the men would love to bellow out the risqué lyrics of the latest music hall songs.

The pub was also a meeting place, a place where the world was put to rights, or wrongs were amplified, the place where events were instigated and organised and later analysed to the nth degree.

Now and again children would sneak in trailing a stoneware jug over the flagstone floor, pushing their way past men's bodies, crawling between their legs. Finding their way through the smoke they would climb the couple of wooden steps provided for the purpose, peer over the counter and ask for the jug to be filled with the warm, dark brown, strong bitter beer that they had been ordered to get and to take home. The publican, his white apron tenting over an extended belly, would supply the foamy liquor and offer the young beer carrier a stick of rock from a candy jar kept under the bar. The jug was heavy but not so heavy that the sweet could not be consumed on the way home, diluting the temptation of an inquisitive child sampling for themselves the contents of the jug. Jack had completed this errand many times when he was smaller, and had not always avoided that temptation.

Edward elbowed his way to the bar and ordered their usual two pints of the local brew, Burtons bitter, in handled glass mugs. When he returned Jack was already in conversation with Joshua Tindale, father of the recently deceased twins. Joshua had his hand on Jack's shoulder, unsteady on his feet from the number of liquid condolences he had already been offered and consumed.

'They were good lads really,' he slurred, 'Had to take the belt to them now and then, but that's how it is with lads isn't it. I used to get a good leathering from me own dad and hasn't done me no harm. Maybe I was too soft on them, let them run around wild a bit too often.'

'It was a terrible accident,' said Jack, 'nowt that anybody could have done about it. Our little brother George got on well with your lads and I'm sure he'll miss them.'

'You know the worst of it is that in another couple of years they'd have been earning. A bit more money coming into the house would have done us no harm, that's for sure,' Joshua paused, peering into the far distance, 'Dammit! You work so much, you have plans you know, you get so close to something better and then it's bloody snatched away in a minute. Damn, damn, damn.'

'Would you like another drink, Joshua?' asked Edward, 'Get you a whisky perhaps?'

'No Edward, I can feel myself going. I know I've had too much already. Thanks all the same, I'd better be getting home.'

Joshua turned and headed for the street but before he got to the door he was waylaid by two more of his neighbours who put their arms around his shoulders and led him, with little complaint, back to the bar.

Jack and Edward shook their heads.

Adam Thompson, a fellow footballer, was close by and Jack called him over.

Like Edward, Adam was a hewer. A well-built young man he lived on his own and was obsessed by three passions; pigeon racing, fishing and football. A broad smile on his face Adam offered to buy Jack and Edward a drink and handed them each a cigarette. Such generosity showed that Adam was not short of a bob or two and Jack assumed it was because he had been working the softer part of the “Baggy” seam that week.

Unlike the brothers, who had been born in the colliery town, Adam was a relative newcomer with no other family. A relatively quiet man, he opened up when you got to know him and was certainly hard working. Not even the underground shift supervisors could find fault with his effort.

'I've just been told where there's good fishing for trout,' confided Adam, 'but it's not exactly free access.'

Keen fisherman were not averse to a bit of trespassing when there was good sport to be had and although it was treated with humour it was a pretty serious offence if you got caught.

Jack wasn't interested in fishing so he ignored the comment.

'You ready for the game tomorrow?'

Adam didn't seem to mind. He was equally passionate about football.

'Going to be a tough game,' he said.

'Oh no,' said Edward butting in, 'you guys are going to get boring about football now. I'll leave you to it,' and he started to walk away towards the piano, 'Jack I'll catch up with you later, we'll walk back together.'

Edward liked to sing and had a rich baritone of which he was quite proud. The gaggle of men around the piano made room for him. Edward knew most of the words of the music hall song they were singing and joined in the chorus enthusiastically,

I was holding me coconut,
when a lady winked at me,
I see you've got it with you,
she shouted out with glee.
Up came a policeman,
he threw me in the cut,
the only thing that held me up,
was holding on to me coconut.

Singing always made him smile.

Sam Hudson, Anne's father, was at the bar. A large, sour man he was still dirty, having come straight from the pit-head to the pub. Sam did not pass on his pay to his wife Ruth but gave her an allowance to eke out on food, clothing, and all the other household essentials.

Ruth was well known to her neighbours for scrounging a little bit of this and a little bit of that to make ends meet and she explained away the cuts and bruises that were sometimes evident on the little flesh she exposed by saying that she was a clumsy woman, always bumping into something or tripping over something else. The walls of the houses were thin enough for neighbours to hear other causes, but a man's home was his castle and no one felt it their place to interfere.

Sam kept the rest of the money for himself, feeling that he'd earned it and with only one child at home he may as well spend it.

Over the years there had been the odd course remark about Sam's lack of fertility, particularly as his one success had turned out to be a girl. But as he had a violent temper that was easily sparked it was a brave man who would say anything to his face. He was, above all other things, an obsessive gambler. Horses, dogs, pigeons, football scores were all the same to him. If there was a good bet to be had, good odds and the prospect of some good winnings then Sam was up for it. He was the loudest of a close-knit group of hard drinking, hard working, hard living men and his drunkenness and aggression regularly got him into trouble, most of it of his own making.

Sam's voice rose loud above the singing. He pushed and shoved his way to where Jack and Adam were still in serious discussion about the best tactics for tomorrow's football game, Jack playing down the right wing and Adam as centre forward.

Sam barged in between them. With his face only inches away from Adam's he glared at him accusingly.

'You bastard,' he said, 'that bloody bird of yours was a dead cert. You did a deal didn't you? Held her back from the clock, bet against your own. Made yourself some good money I'll be bound and took bastards like me for fools.'

Adam's prize pigeon, Caesar, a favourite in the previous weekend's races had unaccountably failed to show.

Adam stood his ground.

'It happens,' he said and turned his back to walk away.

Sam was having none of this. With a couple of his hefty chums at his back egging him on and fuelled by the large amount of beer he'd supped already, he was up for a fight. He reached out a coal-blackened hand, grabbed Adam by the shoulder and gruffly swung him around.

'You're not getting away with it that easy,' he growled.

As the exchange grew more heated it attracted attention. The piano music faded and more eyes turned towards the two protagonists. Sam normally provided good entertainment when he was riled.

'Get your hands off me,' said Adam, keeping his voice calm and even, although there was no mistaking the underlying grit.

Jack tried to intervene but Adam waved him back with his free arm.

'I can handle this,' he said, 'Now Mr Hudson what exactly is your problem?'

'I want everybody to hear,' shouted Sam, 'I'm calling you a cheat, Adam Thomson. A cheat and a liar. You know as well as I do that that bird of yours is a champion and should have won easy. You held it back. I know you did!'

'You must be mad,' Adam was beginning to lose his own temper now, 'I've never cheated in a race and I never will. Why would I?'

'You knew I was betting on your bird. You did it to spite me, to make me look daft.'

'You do a grand job of that without any help from me,' barked Adam, 'Look at yourself man, you've had too much to drink. Get yourself home before you start to regret it.'

'I'm not going to regret this ...' said Sam and swung his clenched fist in a haymaker of a blow. The blow never landed, it was deflected aside by a smaller, cleaner man, deceptively strong, who now stood between the two combatants.

Gabriel Hall was a surface worker. Good at maths at school he had risen from underground work to become one of the colliery's financial clerks. His job was to tally the hours that men worked and to convert the hours into pay. Although the underground workers resented the cushy jobs of the office personnel and were suspicious of their closeness to management it was not in anybody's interests to fall out with Gabriel, his hands were too close to the purse strings. Gabriel knew who was down the pit, when and for how long. He was a man that it would be best to cultivate as a friend. It amused Gabriel that people were so particularly nice to him and that some of the men had creative but lame and ultimately unsuccessful explanations as to why their hour tally had somehow been undercounted. He was always clean and neatly dressed and was one of the best boxers in the colliery village.

'I think that's enough now,' he said, getting hold of Sam, 'I think you've given enough entertainment for one evening,' and then to everybody, but nobody in particular, 'OK, the show's over.'

Sam stayed silent but continued to glare at Adam who held his gaze.

Slowly but surely the attention of the onlookers drifted, the piano started playing again, the sound of singing, led by Edward's baritone, again filled the room. Gabriel took Sam by the arm.

'I'm just off home now Sam,' he said, 'why don't you walk with me. You know how scared we surface workers are of the dark.'

'I'm up for a bit of fresh air,' said Jack, 'mind if I come along?'

Once outside in the cool night air Sam Hudson slouched morosely, glaring at the ground. He swayed as he walked, supported on either side by Gabriel and Jack.

'You'll never bloody learn will you Sam,' said Jack.

'He's cheated me out of me money,' answered Sam, 'there's time yet to get me own back.'

It was a clear night and the moon was high, lighting their way. Behind them the red glow of the coke ovens gave a false sense of a sunset or a dawn that never rose nor set.

On reaching Sam's house, Gabriel lent across and whispered into his ear.

'Just one more thing Sam. It wouldn't be sensible for a man to take out any frustrations he might have on others weaker than himself. No Sam, such a man might just be getting himself into more trouble. Wouldn't be sensible at all. You do understand me, don't you Sam.'

Sam shook himself loose and walked towards the door of his house. The back lit head and shoulder silhouettes of his wife and daughter could be clearly seen peeping through the front room curtains.

Anne saw Jack. She hung her head and turned away. She knew her mother would need help to get her father washed and into bed. She was just hoping he wouldn't be too difficult.

When Jack returned to the Barley Mow, Adam had already left. Their conversation on the best football tactics would now have to wait for another time. Edward subtly mentioned that the singing was making his throat dry and Jack brought in the appropriate remedy in two pint glasses.

They left the pub as Joshua Tindale was staggering to the exit for the umpteenth time. They helped him to finally make his escape and walked him home through the gaslit streets, their hobnailed boots scraping and scrunching on the cobbles. Joshua leaned heavily on Edward and when they pushed open his front door and shouted in, Mrs Tindale asked if Edward and Jack could help get Joshua to bed as in her pregnant condition it was beyond her. Jack and Edward obliged, passing the twin's sheet covered bodies which still lay in the corner, silent observers to the scene, as they maneuvered their father towards the stairs.

Only a game

Joe, Jack's father, looked up from his breakfast plate.

'Sounds like a lot of goings on in the pub last night lads,' he said to Jack and Edward, who along with Mary, George and grandpa Wallace were gathered round the kitchen table, eating.

'Storm in a teacup I think,' said Jack, 'You know how Sam Hudson gets when he's got a bevvy or two inside of him.'

'Aye well, like as not he's got a few things to worry about. There's rumours of shifts and mebbe even jobs being cut back. Stocks are too high apparently, prices too low, the normal crap you hear before the axe begins to fall. And Sam's not too popular, could be one of the first in line for the chop.'

Jack's father was a simple, straightforward man. He worked hard, kept his nose clean and expected nothing more than a fair day's pay for a fair day's work. If he could keep a roof over his family's head, food on the table and clothes on their backs then he was satisfied. A family man at heart he had no real ambitions of his own. He and Mary had come here as newlyweds in search of work and a home. It had been a time of the sinking of new shafts in the colliery, creating new jobs, and houses were on offer. They had grabbed at the opportunity. If his own heart was anywhere other than wherever his family was, it was farther north where he was born and raised, where granite hills rose from river cut valleys and you could breathe deep, filling your lungs with fresh air, crisp and fragrant as the heather underfoot.

When Joe did think of his northern world the sun was always shining, the sky was always blue. When not working underground in the safety lamp lit murk of the coalface he would willingly help grandpa, Mary's father, with the allotment and in particular he liked the chickens, who's clucking and head-jerking antics would make him smile. They never seemed to quite know where they were and each time they raised their heads to look around they seemed startled, as if they were seeing the place for the first time and wondering how they'd got there.

When in need of solace he would take long solitary walks, away from the grime and into the surrounding green, climbing and gazing at far horizons. Atop a summit he would simply sit, eat the bait Mary had prepared for him and look to the sky, watching the clouds float by. He would return refreshed and ready for another day. He would never talk to anybody about these walks. There was nothing to say.

Joe had his own prejudices when it came to recognising the difference between owners and workers though and he was not shy in repeating them around the kitchen table.

'No matter about the volatility of the coal prices the bosses'll always keep their big houses and lots of servants to keep them going. And their missuses have got to have their fur coats and jewellery and the latest fashion. I feel for them, it must be really starting to pinch,' he said sarcastically.

'But you'll still touch your cap to them in the street won't you Dad,' said Edward.

Joe always rose to his son's baiting, 'Got to keep a roof over our heads don't I, and food on the table. Stand up to them individually and they just break you, next thing you know you're out on the street, no house, no food and no job. If you're going to stand up to these bastards you need to do it as part of a crowd, that's were the union comes in.'

Jack rolled his eyes, he wasn't in the mood for another of his father's well-ploughed rants on the Union and the merits of membership.

'When will we know about the job cuts?' he asked.

'God only knows, they normally save it up for just before Christmas to get us in the festive mood,' said his father.

'Can't you talk about something a bit more cheerful,' said Mary, starting to clear away the dirty dishes and put them into the kitchen sink.

'You coming to watch me play football?' asked Jack.

'Would like to son,' said Joe, glancing across at Mary, 'but me and your mam have got something else on this afternoon. Hope you have a good game, and don't get yourself injured. Can't afford the loss of pay at this time of uncertainty.'

'Thanks for caring dad,' said Jack.

'Me and George'll come along,' said grandpa, 'swell the crowd a bit, give you a cheer.'

'You better score a goal or two,' said George, 'give 'em a good hiding.'

The field used for the inter-village football games was at the back of the schoolhouse, alongside the allotments. The seriousness with which the game was taken was apparent in the precision with which the pitch was measured out at a regulation 100 yards long and 50 wide. The goalposts were 8 yards apart, the bar 8 feet from the ground. The woodwork was maintained a brilliant white by dedicated supporters, using paint that had somehow materialised from the colliery storehouse. There was no net.

Jack played on the right wing for the colliery team, with Adam Thompson centre forward. The nearby village of Langley Mill supplied their opponents and an intense rivalry existed between the two teams. To prevent exagerated home bias, about which there had been many pub-grumbled accusations after previous games, the referee was also from Langley Mill and was expected to know better than to attempt any obvious lean towards his own team if he wished to return home from this hostile territory still in one piece. Indeed he was loudly reminded of the fact by some of the roughest fraction of the home crowd, Sam Hudson prominent amongst them, as the teams ran out onto the pitch. He waved back jauntily, but the worried look on his face showed that he'd taken the point.

The thin crowd lined the side of the pitch, opposing supporters on opposite sidelines, a smell of stale ale and smoke exuding from most of the men. Only a few of the women were in attendance and they formed a rather more attractive and cleaner clique to one end of the home crowd. Anne Hudson stood in amongst the other young women, although her mother Ruth had stayed at home to avoid the embarrassment of hearing the foul language that came so loud and liberally from her husband's mouth. Some of the younger girls giggled behind their hands as they scrutinised some of the player's physiques.

The home team goalkeeper was a tall, cool, clearheaded player who could be relied upon to withstand the inevitable bullying that would come from the opposing team's forwards. The two full backs had been selected for their pugnacious strength and resolve and as part of a 5 man defence they were under clear instructions to play it safe, do nothing fancy, not to worry about where the ball went but just to get it out of the danger area as quickly and effectively as possible. More centrally the three halfbacks were to support their forwards, or tackle back, winning back the ball and feeding it through the mid-field in wave after wave of offensive play designed to grind the enemy into submission. The mid-field and attackers would be working together to get a shot on goal, getting the ball to Adam whenever he was in a good shooting position. The wide players, with Jack on the right, would run their wings, dribbling the ball down the touchline and delivering pinpoint crosses into the penalty area for more centrally placed players to head or hammer past the helpless goalie and into the goal. Well at least that was the plan.

The men knew that they had to play together as a team if they were going to win and through experience and training they had come to know each other's ways. Each would try to play to his team-mate's strengths, whilst aware of and covering their weaknesses. The team trained and practiced twice a week when they could, shifts and weather permitting.

A football injury was a serious thing, leading to a man having to take time off work, a loss of pay and a lack of any sympathy from around his own kitchen table. Once a game had started however this did not prevent the men from playing hard, holding nothing back.

Thus were the positions, thus the training, thus the tactics.

In the back room of the Barley Mow Gabriel Hall, who helped with the training and the management of the team, would make it all seem so easy, their plan so perfect, no margin for error, an unstoppable force, an invincible team. Clearly no one could stand against them. They had the best players, all previous disappointments could be put down to experience. The Langley Mill team could not beat them, they stood no chance, they were lambs to the slaughter.

But Gabriel Hall was not on the sidelines for this particular game and now, as the whistle blew to begin the game, they were not so sure.

The pitch was heavy with recent rain and the surface cut up badly under Jack's half inch studs sending pieces of green sod flying and leaving furrowed scars behind. When Jack first got the ball he was immediately scythed to the ground by the opposing full-back, a vicious brute, short, stocky, and built like a brick wall. As the heavy leather ball flew out for a throw-in he tugged on Jack's shirt and growled into his face.

'I hope you've said your bloody prayers mate, I'm taking no fucking prisoners.'

Jack smiled back, 'We'll just have to see about that won't we,' he said.

Grandpa Wallace and George stood on the sidelines shouting encouragement. Anne had her hands to her mouth.

As the game progressed Jack was repeatedly and unceremoniously upended each time the ball came to him, tackled from behind in blatant but un-penalised flagrance of the rules of the game. He winced as he picked himself up and limped on.

'I'll take your fucking leg off next time,' was all the sympathy that was shouted in his ear.

Jack remonstrated with the referee that he had been fouled and was supported in his claims from the sidelines.

'Are you bloody blind as well as daft,' bellowed Sam at the referee, 'you're on borrowed time mate.'

Beyond this private duel the game flowed evenly from end to end, the home goalkeeper being forced into a number of brave saves.

Whether influenced by the verbal chastisement or not, the next time that Jack was chopped to the floor the referee awarded a free-kick and shook his finger theatrically from side to side in the direction of the offending full-back, who just smiled back unabashed.

As the free-kick was about 20 yards from goal the opposing team formed a wall of three players 6 yards from the ball. The referee blew his whistle but instead of shooting Jack chipped the ball into the centre of the penalty area where Adam rose to head it confidently into the top corner scoring the first and only goal of the half.

Anne knew what she wanted to do and as the half-time interval would only be five minutes long she knew she had to take her chance quickly. As inconspicuously as she could she made her way over to where the opposing team were gathered in a huddle. Sidling up to the offending full-back, she whispered something to him. Startled, his mouth fell open, but before he had time to collect his wits sufficiently to respond to Anne, she had turned her back and walked away.

The second half brought an early equaliser, the ball played long into the penalty area where it was chested down and, giving the goalkeeper little chance, dispatched firmly into the goal.

The crowd watched a committed second half as it ebbed and flowed. Both teams played for all they were worth, and played as well as they could. It was a fast game and running to a close finish when, much to the exasperation of all, the game was temporarily suspended to clear an escaped chicken from the pitch, an embarrassed grandpa Wallace disappearing with the offending bird in the direction of the allotments.

Although the full-back continued to play a strong game he had pulled back from his former level of viciousness and Jack was not forever picking himself up off the ground. Occasionally the full-back would glance in Anne's direction and she would nod back.

In the final minutes of the game Jack, buoyed by the much easier time he was having of it in the second half, centred to Adam who hammered a shot goalwards, beating the goalkeeper but not the crossbar. The ball crashed against the woodwork knocking it off and rebounded onto the chest of the officious full-back from where it bounced tamely back and despite frantic efforts, over the line. The referee looked around uncertainly but as the ball had clearly entered the goal well under bar level he had no alternative but to award the score. It was an own goal and although the referee allowed an uncomprehendingly long period of extra time beyond the allotted 90 minutes, Langley Mill could not respond and the game was won.

After the game Edward, who had noticed Anne's actions during the half-time interval sought her out and asked her what she'd done. Anne confided that she had approached the Langley Mill full-back at half time and said,

'I know what you're up to, and if you don't play the game more fairly I'll tell your woman all about it.'

Edward was flabbergasted and asked how on earth she knew the man, and more importantly how she knew his secrets.

Anne replied that she had never seen him before, had not set eyes on him until today, but that she thought that the kind of man who would cheat so blatantly on the football field would be very likely to be also cheating off it. She had also noted a woman standing on the touchline who cheered him on, so had guessed that was probably his wife. From the man's reaction she had clearly hit a nerve, her hunch had been correct.

Edward laughed. He thought it was a great story.

'I'd better watch out for you,' he said.

Elated by this reaction, Anne sought out Jack and told him. Jack's reaction was very different.

'I already have one mother, I don't need another,' he said angrily.

Jack felt his manhood had been challenged. That somehow his ability to cope had been questioned. He was a man and didn't need this kind of help from a girl.

Anne was very upset by Jack's reaction and tried immediately to apologise and explain but Jack would not listen, he turned his mud-smeared back and walked away.

Edward caught up to him and, putting an arm round his shoulders, calmed him down.

'You're my brother Jack, and I love you,' he said, 'but you're also an idiot.'

Jack's temper was like a firecracker, quick to flare but soon burnt out. He looked around for Anne, saw her slinking away and ran after her to apologise. He'd never had any woman, except his own mother, stick up for him before, there must be a reason.

Anne turned and waited for him to catch her up.

Jack's mother and father had not been at the game. Instead they were standing side-by-side in a church yard with their heads bowed towards a headstone at the foot of which flowers had been laid.

'I've never been very lucky with daughters,' said Mary, wiping her eyes on her uplifted apron.

The child had been stillborn and now Mary could not have any more children. They had named her Sarah after Mary's own mother. They had moved to the area for the work but they had settled, had made a home and created a family here. Two of their children had been born in the village, although one had died, and they couldn't remember the last time they'd been anywhere else. Maybe this is where they would stay.

'You'll make a good mother-in-law when the time comes,' said Joe, 'there's daughters out there don't know what's coming.'

Mary smiled and arm-in-arm in their Sunday best they walked away, passing by two freshly covered graves on their way out of the graveyard. The mounds were a dark brown and close together, as the twins had always been in life, and on top of each there was a Robin, one singing, the other picking worms from the freshly turned soil.

Skin deep

It was a sun-bright day as grandpa Wallace made his familiar slow meandering way to the allotments. As was his habit he paused frequently for a word here or a nod there to the familiar faces, a deep rumbling chuckle never far from his lips, the sound made rounder through the filter of his carefully tended nicotine stained whiskers.

When he reached his own plot he gave a cursory inspection to the leeks and cabbages, standing to attention in their agricultural lines, to ensure that they were not under any new form of attack from insect, mould or bacteria, then went and knelt by a cleared and prepared but unplanted area of deep loam.

As he stooped he could feel the sun burning down on his thinning grey-haired head, the heat bringing back flashes of memory from former days, half a world away. He paused while images of bleached waist high grass played in his head and he narrowed his eyes involuntarily as his mind watched for a glimpse of black skin momentarily appearing between the stalks. He strained to hear beyond the perpetual swish of the veldt wind, listening for the human made rustle that would spark the change from sweat trickling anticipation to adrenaline fuelled soldier drilled action. His head swam, he wondered idly if it were today's heat or yesterday's memories that made him feel dizzy.

Grandpa Wallace rolled up his shirt sleeves exposing the faded vein blue tattoos and reached forward to place his outspread fingers onto the warm, dark, surface of the soil, as if feeling for the heartbeat of the fertile earth under his palms. Smiling he pushed his fingers deeper.

The dizziness that he had felt before had subsided, to be replaced by a deep, resonant pounding that filled his ears and excluded all other sounds. It was so all encompassing that it was simultaneously both everything and nothing. The pulsing filled his head but at the same time his consciousness ignored it and he pushed his fingers downward, feeling the black moist warmth of the earth. As he looked down **her face** appeared between his hands. Black, African. He tried to scoop her up, to hold her tenderly, tears welling in his rheumy eyes.

'I did mean to return,' he whispered, 'but I was only young, too young, too full of myself and too stupid to understand. Big soldier in a red uniform.'

Grandpa Wallace looked into the deep brown eyes, searching for forgiveness or at least a degree of understanding. 'We could hardly communicate. They would have killed you if they'd known. It wasn't right. Black and white don't mix. But they did for us during those few short weeks. I was killing your people and loving you at the same time. It was impossible.'

The pounding in grandpa Wallace's head now became a whooshing, liquid swirling pressure that built so that he gasped as though he were starting to drown.

But he did not wish to surface. Not anymore.

The surf rose, the waves crashed into sparks that flew before his eyes. The face that he held in his hands began to dissolve back into earth.

A final tide rushed towards him, red as blood, mellow as sunset. Then it was upon him,

'I'm s...,'

Red erupted before his eyes and a tired old body that was no longer grandpa Wallace fell forward, well tended whiskers merging with the rich soil.

It was three hours or so later that the body was found, the sun having had time to burn the back of the corpse's neck and outstretched forearms scarlet. On the right arm a faded blue name stood proud against the red. A girl's name, African and unpronounceable. Mary's first action on being called to her father's body was to roll down the sleeve and hide the tattoo from the light.

Keep on keeping on

The rum ration, dispensed from large SRD stamped stone jars, was quickly consumed. The black treacle thick liquid enflamed courage as it roughly burnt a hot course down Jack's throat, sending tendrils of warmth to the tips of his toes, to the centre of his consciousness. Amidst the thunderous, earth trembling noise of the artillery barrage the men lined up in the trench stood in silence. The metal clad heads drooped and waited, waited. Anxiety was a taste in dry mouths, the smell was of cordite, old gas, urine and fear. Eyes were glazed and fixed on the rough, mud soaked sacking of sandbags, focused on infinity.

Time jested with them maliciously as it slowed to a crawl, the next moment coming in time with their heartbeat, equally awaited and dreaded. The waiting, the tick, tick, tick of the tedious seconds was almost worse than the anticipation of the cruel action ahead, almost - but not.

The shrill note of the whistle when it came was small, plaintively insignificant, and mainly unheard. The shout from men in khaki rippled along the line as bodies began to move, to haul themselves up the thin wooden slats of the trench ladders, over the parapet edge, breaking the skyline, standing exposed and fragile.

Stepping through their own lines of defensive barbed wire, gaps cut in the night, they stumbled clumsily.

But this barbed tangle was not the problem. The problem was the world of screaming, smoking death that they walked into, where all sound was at full volume, beyond the ability to cope, deafening all.

Jack's mind screeched to him to stop, to turn back, to fall, to feign injury, to survive. To his left an officer was waving his pistol, his mouth moving, shouting urgent encouragement, but the sound was lost in the clamour. Jack walked forward, the mud grasping at his ankles. It was as if the earth was trying to purposely grab at him and slow his progress, to hold him back or hold him steady, to make him an easy target.

Heavily laden, he carried an SMLE rifle, bayonet affixed, and a back-pack with trench shovel, .303 ammunition and Mills grenades in place of food and forks. Around him he saw his comrades start to fall. Fear trickled down the back of his neck, his temples pounding. His mind cried up to the heavens.

'Oh God, help me get through this. Help me not to turn and flee. There is so much now that I wish that I had done. So much I would do if I'm given the chance. God, the fates or lucky chance protect me, let me live.'

12 inch shells are hurled impersonally into the chaos from a railway siding 2 miles away. There are so many guns firing that three shells a second are falling, some are shrapnel shells designed to maim and maul human flesh, some high explosive. The high explosive hurls the barbed wire high into the air but does not cut it and it returns to earth more tangled and impenetrable than it was before. Lessons

learnt from previous barrages meant that few shells are misdirected or fall short, killing those they were meant to protect.

Anaesthetised with adrenaline the diminishing numbers continue forward. The bodies strewn in the mud are only pieces of meat now, looked upon only as you would look upon a butcher's slab, running red. No man's land is churned brown and bloody, uneven, sticky, pockmarked with shell holes half full with putrid water. Severed, shredded body parts are scattered untidily, legless feet are still in their shoes, snake coils of disembowelled intestines slick the surface. But such sites have been seen before and old carcasses, whose chest cavities are home to families of rats, have been the source of the smell, taste and sights that the men who occupy the front line trenches have grown used to, desensitised by a saturation of familiarity.

In a different, recent, time, now completely out of mind, Jack and the men of his platoon, his battalion, had trekked from the reserve lines, marched along dirt roads in tidy line and file, swinging arms, waving at the curious French civilians who stood at the side of the road or looked up from rickety horse-drawn carts.

Pack up your troubles in your old kit bag,
and smile, smile, smile,
while you've a lucifer to light your fag,
smile, boys, that's the style.
What's the use of worrying,
it never was worthwhile,
so pack up your troubles in your old kit bag,
and smile, smile, smile.

The singing had helped the time pass, cemented camaraderie and lightened the heart. Gaps in the singing were punctuated by ribald shouts and chatter,

'I'm going to get me a French girl when we get back next time,' shouted Edward to Jack.

'And I'm a monkey's uncle,' said Jack.

It was somehow easy to forget the men they had known in life, that they had buried, that they had picked up lifeless as logs, cursing their weight, the flotsam from the casualty clearing station. They had probably been just like them, hoping for a “blighty”, but now they were in the ground and easily forgotten. There was thankfully little time to think, to digest what was happening. Events piled upon events too quickly, there was too much to take in, and maybe that was a blessing.

When they had left the town behind them skylarks had called from above the gently rolling farmland through which they had marched. That evening everything was red. The sun set red, the rivers and wet roads and pools reflected back a red answer. The ground they entered was stained red and in the verges the poppies, the poppies danced.

Jack did not hear the shell. He was aware only of a blinding light and the searing red-hot ripping pain in his leg. The shock wave lifted him bodily and flung him cart-wheeling up, and then limply down, down onto the mud and into the mess and a personal blackness.

Is this death? In the blackness it was warm and comforting, all his problems large or small were over, over forever. Even the feeling, the awareness of the blackness and of the warmth of the blackness, began to drift away.

An unknowable gulf of time later sharp searing pain drew Jack back. The return of pain was cold, hard, and bitter. 'Why?' he thought, 'Let me return to the pain-free blackness. Is this hell?' Jack vaguely wondered if he had entered purgatory to atone for his sins. His head was buzzing, he lay on his belly in soaking mud.

As semi-consciousness returned he instinctively reached out, searching for a safe haven. Hand over hand he clawed at the slippery surface dragging his numbed, unhelpful body after. He had no sense of location nor direction, but simply an urgent, compelling need to be less exposed. As he slithered across the ground he left a slime trail in his wake that was streaked with a red that he could not see, from a wound that he could not feel. His sight was blurred, his hearing full of the noises in his own head. He relied entirely on a sense of feel as he groped around for a shell hole.

He knew he was hurt. His world had collapsed in on him and he felt alone. The world outside the reach of his fingertips had no longer any meaning, it was completely beyond his comprehension and of no consequence. The mud clung on to him, holding him, claiming possession of his mind and body, telling him he was better here, it would keep him safe, warm, comfortable, if only he would listen and stay, and stop, and sleep.

But Jack continued to claw onwards and the earth had pity and he slid down, head first, into a waterlogged shell hole.

With much effort he twisted and rolled himself around and onto his back. He lay gasping, gazing upwards, upwards into a clean, clear, blue, white flecked sky.

'Why am I given the ability to watch my own decline?' he thought.

This seems the cruellest trick of all. Is it not better to have no sense of self, to live only in the minute, conscious only of the now? Better to have no comprehension of self or past or future and to wallow only in the pain, all else forgotten.

He closes his eyes against the sun and looks through translucent blood red lids. It is like being back in the womb. He hears in his ears the dull beating drum of his own pulse, feels the protection of a floating, closed in freedom. Here there is nothing to fear, this world is calm, new and full of amniotic hope. Memory flows like water through his mind. Babbling and turbulent, good and bad, happy and sad, smooth, rough, fast, slow float-bobbing and then swirling, deeper, in the undercurrents. But it does not matter as long as it holds his attention, keeps him awake, stops him from falling asleep. He must not fall asleep. He knows that it is death to fall asleep.

'I am in no man's land. I am swimming in my own gore. There is a drizzling rain but there is blue in the sky. I am sure I am dying. What sadistic devil then, within all this chaos causes my nose to run? Is it a prank? Above all else this tickle annoys me. I can feel the hairs rise on my upper lip to catch the flow. I pout to try to defy gravity. I do not want to use my tongue. I do not want the taste in my mouth. My eyes roll in my head and ... and I start, to laugh. To be here, to be in this, like this, and to be worried about a runny nose! Praise the gods for a sense of humour!'

His fingers inch their way across slick wet khaki. Dirty nails, that his mother would have scolded him for, slowly worm across his chest. Unseeing he navigates by touch. He spies out the terrain by fingertip, he concentrates so as not to be lead down false pleats or confuse a tear for a pocket flap. His eyes are focused on infinity as his conscious brain usurps the all-encompassing attention of physical pain to focus his energy, all of his will, into the fingers of his left hand.

Crawling spider-like across his own chest he passes his still beating, pumping heart. His first goal is small, circular, cold and made of brass. He knows that it's close. He knows that his fingers will be able to distinguish the hard circumference, sniff out the cold dimpled smoothness of the surface if he can only get within striking distance. Like a blind man reaching out into a half remembered room, stumbling, sweeping the three-dimensional space in front of his blind eyes, he lifts a finger. It moves from side to side, sensing. He wishes he had an eye on the end of that finger. He focuses on the finger, on the movement, he feels the metal, the brass button, not polished now. Slowly, painfully he unbuttons the pocket, his fingers creep inside.

'I am cold,' he thinks, 'I am cold. My thoughts are becoming cold. I want to sleep and must not sleep. I must keep my eyes open. I must move. Act.'

But he is tired.

'If I died in this shell hole, if I allowed myself to die, if I could reach for my gun and put a bullet through my own brain, no one would know, no one would care. There is nothing special about this shell hole, there is nothing special about me, there is nothing special about any of this.'

In the world around him there is so much death. So many deaths that one more would make no difference. It surrounds him, he is submerged in it, drowning in the decay.

He knows his mother would miss him. Although she never said so he knows that she loves him. His father he couldn't read, he was a man's man but he worked for the family, he provided a roof over their heads, food on the table, clothes on their backs - he had to respect that, and he does.

He feels the lice in his uniform, concentrated in the seams, irritating his skin. Irritation that had mattered before but is now overwhelmed by the waves of this other pain that is so great that it almost makes him laugh. He remembers his younger brother's fascination with these wingless parasitic insects and his pride in remembering their Latin name. He thinks of George. He is growing fast, showing a talent for mathematics. He hopes his younger brother will avoid the pit. With the help of Gabriel Hall perhaps he can be trained in accounts, get the chance of a job in a bank perhaps, above ground and clean.

It is most painful when he thinks about Anne. She has become special to him. He had wanted a life with her however hard it would have been. She deserved a better life. They would have pulled together, they would have created a family. He would have loved her. He does love her.

'So now what if it is my turn,' he thinks, 'isn't this what I've always wanted? To die a hero's death, or at least to die as a soldier, away from home. Isn't this what all my grandfather's stories were about, my games, my training? Isn't it what really, deep down, everyone expected to happen even when we pretended to hope that it would only happen to others? They knew I was not immune didn't they, not immortal, and reading the news, seeing the other houses getting the telegrams, they knew that it was only a matter of time before my time would come.'

He raises the photograph that he has taken from his pocket in front of his eyes. His vision is blurred but he can make out the figure, the smiling face of Anne. He thinks of the others; Edward, George, grandpa, father, mother, his friends. He wonders what they would do in his place. He wonders how they would act if he were gone.

Now on the edge, he chooses to fight to live. He might not be good enough but he will do his best. All he has to do is survive, survive long enough...

He knows there are no promises, maybe he will die anyway. But even then, to die trying is still the better choice. He knows he cannot relive what has already been lived but he wants more. He looks at the photograph. He'll try and get back to Anne.

He'll do his best to get back.

He has never cried as a man. He has been taught that men do not cry. Now here alone in the shell hole, where no one can see him, he cries, sobs his heart out, and for a few precious moments he cannot control his weeping.

With his determination to live the pain increases but now he knows he needs to survive long enough to be found, for the stretcher bearers to carry him out. He wipes away the tears. The cold is getting to him, he needs to find a way to not be there, to distract his body and mind from this reality whilst staying awake. He thinks about his grandfather and his stories. He remembers how they transported him to other places, how time seemed to pass so quickly ...

He closes his eyes so that he can see the boy more clearly.
Just as the eye completes a picture that is not complete so his mind seeks to complete a memory.

It was a warm summer afternoon in the valley. Wild flowers lifted their showy heads above the green blanket and nodded in yellows and reds and blues. The red poppies rose highest, their black hearts beating to the rhythm of their single day in the sun ...

ACKNOWLEDGEMENTS

Thanks to all those who have given me the support and constructive criticism that has got me this far - it has meant a lot!

Versions of two of these stories “Two rooms” and “All in the Jeans” also appear in the Crime & Publishment Anthology *Happily Never After* (2016) and versions of “How to make Spaghetti Bolognese” and “A welcome distraction” in the 2018 Anthology *Wish You Weren’t Here.*

ABOUT THE AUTHOR

John S. Langley was born and raised in the North East of England. He has two brothers, three sons, and one wife. He lives in Cumbria and he and his wife share their home with two cats, four chickens and about 20,000 bees.

Qualified as a Chemical Engineer he had his first career working for large multinational companies, travelling the world at their expense, before moving into consultancy and latterly being his own company.

He has written all his life but the rigours of adhering to the rules of technical report writing put a dampener on creativity and it is only now, before it is too late, that he has returned to his first love and is willing to admit to being an author and poet.

www.ingramcontent.com/pod-product-compliance
Lightning Source LLC
Chambersburg PA
CBHW030334310726
48979CB00001B/24

* 9 7 8 1 9 9 9 6 6 7 6 7 2 *